I0772746

YEAR OF THE RAT

A DOM REILLY MYSTERY

MARSHALL THORNTON

ACKNOWLEDGMENTS

A big thank you to: Joan Martinelli, Nathan Bay, Tina and John Bevington, Randy and Valerie Trumbull, Danielle Wolff, Brian Fagan, and Matt Lubbers-Moore.

PROLOGUE

August 8, 1984

"I could do that," his brother said, setting the glass pipe down on the cluttered coffee table. Pointing to the 45-inch projection TV, he meant Ed McMahon, or maybe Dick Clark. The boxes for the new TV and VCR sat next to them. "I could wear a nice suit and talk on TV. I could say lame ass shit."

The girl, whose name was Audrey and sat behind him in his geometry class, said, "You couldn't. You have to have charisma."

"These guys don't have charisma."

"Yeah, they do. I like them."

"Aw, what do you know."

Danny took a small rock out of a baggie and reached for the pipe. The way his brother watched him do it made him say, "I'll get some money. I promise."

"No freeloaders in this house."

"I'll get money."

"Where?"

It was a hard question and soon Danny's attention drifted back to the TV. Some soap opera actress was trying to say 'indefatigable' but couldn't manage it. She tried over and over again, take after take. The three of them giggled over it. They'd taped the show the night before, so they ran it back to the beginning and giggled at it all a second time.

The walls were covered in harvest gold wood paneling, the dirty sofa depicted a fall tableau—a cornucopia of dingy fruits and vegetables, the shag carpet was a fungal brown. The living room looked like the aftermath of a tropical storm and the kitchen was an ongoing lab experiment. But his brother was proud of the place, and Danny was proud of his brother. When their father died, his brother had taken over and everything had gotten better.

"I wouldn't mind being an actress," Audrey said. "Everyone's nice to you if you're an actress."

She lived on the other side of the culvert in a regular house with a foundation and an above ground swimming pool in the back. Her stepfather was kind of shitty and responsible for the fading bruise on her forehead. Her mother did her best not to notice things like that.

Audrey took a hit off the pipe and then danced around the living room. "See? I could be just like Kristy McNichol or Molly Ringwald or Madonna."

"Madonna's a singer not an actress," his brother said.

"So. Maybe I can sing too."

He waited for his brother to tell Audrey she couldn't be an actress or a singer. Sometimes he was mean like that, telling people all the things they didn't want to hear. But then he started to giggle and the two of them giggled at Audrey for a while.

"Is there any more beer?" His brother asked. But before anyone could get up and look, two guys in their late teens walked in.

It was time for a little business.

ONE

February 7, 1996
Wednesday evening

Time is a dead thing. We like to pretend it's not, that it has unique characteristics. That it flies, it crawls, it races, it drags—or it simply slips away. We waste it and fill it and kill it. None of that is true; it's not time, at all. It's our experience of time. It's what we do with time. Time itself is stubbornly invariable. A minute is a minute, no more, no less.

My partner, Ronnie Chen, and I stood impatiently by the host stand —well, he was impatient. It was his dinner party and we were late. La Bohème was a nouveau Italian restaurant with all white tablecloths, heavy silverware, shiny glasses and small, pricey bouquets of pink roses. The walls were glazed in mottled gold and spotted with mediocre paintings that couldn't decide whether to be abstract or impressionist. The stuffy host tried to put us in our place by studying his reservations book while we stood there.

"The reservation is under Chen. Ronnie—oh, never mind. The rest of our party is already here." And with that Ronnie—small, half-Asian and very young—charged across the dining room.

"Sir," the host said behind us, obviously wanting to lead and not follow. I, however, was quite used to following Ronnie from place to place.

"Hello!" Ronnie called out long before we got to the table. "I'm so sorry we're late. Have you been waiting long?"

The rest of our party was a lawyer named Lydia Gonsalez and her husband, a writer's agent I think, named Wayne—no, Dwayne, Whatley. Sitting at a table for four by the window, they smiled and stood as we reached the table.

"I'm so glad you could come out!" Ronnie continued.

"Thank you for inviting us!" Lydia said, matching my boyfriend's enthusiasm. She was a curvaceous woman in her mid-thirties with black satin hair and milky skin. She wore a mannish blue suit that tried but failed to turn her curves into straight lines. Dwayne was trim and blond, attempting to create an East Coast air of private schools and beach-y compounds but failing dismally.

Conversation was small for a few minutes. They'd really just gotten there moments before we did. Hadn't even ordered drinks yet.

"What is everyone reading?" Dwayne asked. "That's my favorite ice-breaker, by the way."

"I'm reading *The Celestine Prophecy*," Ronnie said. "It's so spiritual." It had been on our nightstand for at least a year. I'd never seen him pick it up.

"I'm not really a reader," I volunteered. Ronnie kicked me under the table since I was halfway through *Independence Day* by Richard Ford.

Lydia said, "I like reading about organized crime. I'll read anything along those lines. It's a hobby of mine."

"You like gangs?" I asked.

"Well, no. Mostly I'm interested in the Mafia. The Italian Mafia. Cosa Nostra. The Black Hand. The Outfit. They have a romance the others don't."

"I don't know," I said. "Ending up dead in the trunk of your car doesn't seem all that romantic to me."

"I blame Francis Ford Coppola," her husband said.

She frowned at him and went on, "Of course they're violent, but they also have a real code of honor and a love of family. The other crime syndicates, the cartels, the Russians, they're brutal just for the sake of brutality." Then she cocked her head and asked, "Dominick. Is that Irish or Italian?"

I didn't have time to answer; the waiter came by and Ronnie asked the table, "Should we have wine or do you want cocktails?"

"I would love—" Lydia began but was stopped when her husband placed his hand over hers.

"Wine is fine with us," he said.

"White? Red? Something different with each course?" Ronnie played host.

"Red," Dwayne said. "We'll have a red."

I watched Lydia's face. There was a lot going on there, I just wasn't sure what.

Ronnie ordered: "A bottle of red and another of white. Something midrange. Californian. Absolutely Californian. These two just bought the cutest little California bungalow on Orizaba."

"Actually," Lydia said. "I'll have an Absolut martini, straight up, olive, dry as a bone."

"Oh gosh," Ronnie said. "I'll have one too, then." He always ordered what the client ordered.

"Nothing for me, thank you," I said. "Just water."

We all looked at Dwayne. "I'll stick with the wine, thank you. Red."

The waiter, who was Hispanic and around Ronnie's age, ran off. After an almost imperceptible pout, Dwayne said, "I'm reading *Atlas Shrugged*. One of our clients wants to adapt it, though I can't see why. It's awful." And that, I supposed, was the whole point of his icebreaker.

He went on. "Do you follow the business? Quentin's latest script came across my desk. Not up to his usual standard but it'll get made anyway."

"I adore insider gossip," Ronnie said. He didn't, he was just good at saying the right thing at the right time.

That launched Dwayne and he began to talk about writers and directors I was sure Ronnie had never heard of, despite the fact that he was nodding enthusiastically with each new name.

Lydia smiled at me and said, "Ronnie tells me you used to be a police detective. Where was that?"

I leaned across the table and said, "Um, this is embarrassing. That's something I told him when I was trying to get him into bed."

"So, it's not true?" she asked, sounding dubious.

"Not at all."

Ronnie, who'd been monitoring both conversations, abruptly switched over, leaving Dwayne in the midst of an anecdote about one of his writer's who'd made a fortune selling movie scripts that never became movies. "What do you mean it's not true?"

"I mean it's not true. I just said it so you'd—"

"But I went after you. Not the other way around. He always does that," he said to Lydia. "Makes it sound like he chased me."

"Maybe I just let you think you were chasing me."

He looked at me, mouth slightly open. I thought he might object again, but he looked away and changed the subject. "*What* are you two going to do with your extra bedrooms? And have you decided? Are you going to put in a pool? I think it's so worth it. Resale value."

Lydia laughed, a pleasant sound, like a wind chime. "Ronnie, we just closed on this house. I'm not going to want to move again for decades."

"Don't worry, I'll let you know when it's the right time to trade up."

"I don't know. Things are getting kind of pricey," Dwayne said, grumpy over being interrupted.

"This is nothing. We still haven't recovered from the dip after the Northridge quake. We will soon and then the market is just going to keep going up and up and up. In a couple of years, I'll find you a deal on something bigger."

"Like the one you have?" Lydia asked.

We lived on 2nd Street, two blocks from the ocean, in a five-bedroom Craftsman by an architect who'd once worked for the famous firm of Greene and Greene. The house was over eighty years old and often reminded me of a cranky, demented old man. Ronnie had gotten it for a scandalously low price a year ago—though not low enough that we didn't keep at least one of the extra bedrooms filled with a roommate. I wondered if Lydia had seen the house or just been told about it.

"Exactly," Ronnie said. "Just like our house.

"I imagine we'll be moving back up to Brentwood by that point," Dwayne said.

Lydia frowned at the mention of Brentwood.

"Speaking of Brentwood," he continued. "Did you hear that O.J. Simpson called into a radio station and dedicated a song to his wife? The wife he killed?"

"He was acquitted," Lydia said. "You shouldn't—"

"*You* think he killed her."

"I do, but that's not our system. He had his trial. He was acquitted. We shouldn't say he killed his wife. It wasn't proven."

"I think they proved it," Dwayne said.

"You weren't on the jury."

To us he said, "My wife, the female Perry Mason."

The waiter returned with the cocktails, a busboy behind him holding the bottle of wine. He set the drinks out and then took the bottle of red from the busboy. As he uncorked it, he said to Ronnie, "I've brought you a Napa Valley pinot noir."

"Lovely."

The waiter poured a little of the red into Ronnie's wine glass, but before he could taste it, he said, "Oh let Dom try it. He's a bartender, it's his area."

I thought I heard a little dig in his voice and nearly rolled my eyes. Tasting wine hardly required expertise. The point was to make sure it wasn't vinegar. You really shouldn't send it back simply because you think it's too sweet or too dry. That would be rude. And ignorant.

The waiter poured another tiny splash into my wine glass. I sipped it. It wasn't bad and it wasn't vinegar.

"Very nice," I said. "Thank you."

The waiter tried to pour me a glass, but I held my hand over it. Then he poured Dwayne's glass. The look on his face was definitely put out.

"I'll leave the wine list in case you'd like something else with dinner. Have you had time to look at the menu?"

"No, we have not," Dwayne answered, his tone terse.

"But—we'll have appetizers," Ronnie said, and then ordered from memory. "The calamari, the bruschetta, the polenta—"

"Ronnie stop, I'm on a diet," Lydia said.

"In that case, add a shrimp cocktail."

"All right, I'll get those started," the waiter said, before he and the busboy scurried off.

"So, I guess you're not an alcoholic then," Dwayne said to me.

"I'm sorry?"

"You didn't order a drink. I thought you might be a friend of Bill but then you sampled the wine."

"I don't enjoy drinking as much as I did when I was younger."

"Do you mind my asking how old you are?"

"Dwayne, you're being rude," his wife pointed out.

Of course, I knew what he was really asking, so I said, "I'll save you the math. I'm twenty years older than Ronnie."

"No, you're not. You're sixteen years older than I am. You're forty-four, I'm twenty-eight," my lover insisted. "He says he's good at math, but he's really not."

Dwayne smiled at me as though he'd won something. Then he conceded, "Lydia's right. I suppose it is rude asking people's ages. I apologize."

"Don't worry about it."

We were silent for a long moment.

"This is lovely," Lydia said. I couldn't tell if she meant the martini or the restaurant or the quiet.

"Why Long Beach?" I asked, taking a sip of ice water.

"My office is down here," Lydia said. "On Fourth."

"Horrible neighborhood," Dwayne said.

"But inexpensive," Lydia said.

I had the distinct impression Dwayne's office wasn't anywhere nearby. My guess was Beverly Hills—a very awkward commute.

"Lydia runs The Freedom Agenda," Ronnie told me.

"She's a defense attorney," Dwayne said.

"I'm not exactly a defense attorney."

"Yes, you are," her husband said.

"The Freedom Agenda works to get the unjustly incarcerated out of prison. I only work for the innocent. A defense attorney takes anyone as a client. Guilty or innocent. Usually guilty."

"You still defend people," Dwayne insisted. "You're a defense attorney."

"I don't think of it that way."

There was another long, tense silence.

"I suppose you're planning to be in your new house by the first?" Ronnie said more than asked.

"March fifteenth," Lydia replied. "We got an extension on our lease. I wanted to be able to get painters in and I'm getting rid of that awful vanity in the bathroom."

"Oh, that's a good idea. I didn't want to say anything but—"

"How did the two of you meet?" Dwayne asked, with a hint of 'you don't make sense' still in his voice.

"Oh, I was just wandering around Santa Monica Boulevard one night and there he was, like a present under the Christmas tree." Ronnie was creatively and deceptively telling the truth.

I said, "I told him it was a bad idea, but he didn't believe me."

"You're an adorable couple," Lydia said.

I wasn't sure if even I believed that. It worked for us, though. I just didn't expect other people to see it. And, I wasn't sure how much it mattered.

"Thanks," Ronnie said. Diplomatically he went on, "You two are obviously meant for each other. How did *you* meet?"

Dwayne launched into a well-rehearsed story about being set up by one of the agents in his office on a blind date. They met at a trendy place in West Hollywood, but it turned into one of the worst dates of his life. After his date threw a glass of white wine at him and stomped out, the woman at the next table smirked, then apologized for smirking, then asked what he'd done to deserve the baptism. He said he wasn't sure and asked her help figuring it out.

"And I still have no idea why she did it," Lydia said, recognizing her cue. I wondered how true that was. By this point, she must have an inkling.

The appetizers came and we spent a good five minutes tasting and complimenting them. The conversation drifted to the Whitewater scandal —none of us actually knew why it was a scandal, though Dwayne pretended to—the Oscars, which would be announced soon, and the man Lydia had recently gotten out of prison.

"His name is Jimmy Claxton and he was convicted of raping two women. They both identified him in a line up. That was in the eighties. We have DNA testing now, and there was material to test which proved that it wasn't him. In fact, the women weren't even raped by the same man. He'd served almost eight years."

"That's terrible!" Ronnie said. "Isn't that terrible, Dom."

I nodded and sipped my water. A lemon slice floated on top.

"How could they identify the wrong man?" Ronnie again.

"Witness identifications are notoriously unreliable," Lydia explained, "but juries love them. If a witness says something stridently enough, they'll believe it."

The waiter came back with the busboy. As our appetizer plates were cleared, he asked if we'd like to order. I ordered the lobster ravioli with a Caesar salad, Ronnie had the seafood pasta dish—his usual order—and the bean soup, Dwayne the veal piccata, and Lydia ordered a Caesar salad and asked for a piece of salmon poached but with nothing else—a criminal misuse of a restaurant like La Bohéme.

After the waiter left, she said, "The reason I asked about your being a detective is that I need an investigator."

"I'm sure you'll find someone."

"We could talk about it," she said, though it didn't make a lick of sense.

"I'd need a license, wouldn't I?"

"We can't afford a *licensed* investigator. Most organizations like ours are using law students to do the most outrageous things."

"I have a job. I'm not looking—"

"Three days a week," Ronnie said, giving me the eye. "You'd have time to fit this in. It's perfect for you."

"Why is it perfect for me?"

He frowned at me but didn't answer.

"I wish I only had to work three days a week," Dwayne said.

I ignored him since I was too busy glaring at my lover. "Is this some kind of setup?"

"Of course not. You come to all my client dinners. This one just has a little something extra."

In other words, it was a setup. He and Lydia had cooked this up. Mainly because Ronnie had gotten a wrong idea in his head. I decided not to press the point and turned and smiled at our guests.

"I'm sorry if I overstepped," Lydia said. "It's a crappy job, anyway. I'd be lucky to get you."

"Why?"

She took a breath, stumped for a moment, then said, "Because you ask questions like that."

It was a bullshit answer and I was at a loss to figure out why she was so interested in me. I had no experience and she had no idea if I'd be a good investigator or not. All she had was my boyfriend's recommendation. I made a mental note to strangle him on the drive home.

After a couple of starts and stops, the conversation got back on track. The wine helped. Ronnie ordered a bottle of white and it arrived right as the martinis were finished. They made quick work of the bottle and Ronnie ordered another.

The three of them chatted about a recent movie, *Sense and Sensibility*. I hadn't seen it. Ronnie had gone with his mother, who was his regular Friday night date. Lydia and Ronnie loved the film. Dwayne could only see it in terms of his business.

"I don't know why everyone is so impressed by adaptations. If it's a good enough book it's little more than a typing assignment."

"You loved *Apollo 13*," Lydia said. "Wasn't that based on a book?"

"Was it? I'm not remembering."

None of us believed him. It was his business and he'd already done a good bit of name dropping. He remembered everything. Or at least everything he wanted to.

The salads and soup came and went. The entrées arrived. Everything was perfect, but we knew it would be. I couldn't help doing the math in my head. The entrées alone were nearly a hundred, as were three bottles of wine. We'd probably have dessert, we usually did. At least two to share. Maybe more. The miscellaneous items would bring the total over two-sixty or two-seventy. Plus the tip. Ronnie always tipped at least fifty, sometimes more.

Over three hundred dollars for dinner was extravagant, but the house they'd bought was nearly three hundred thousand. Ronnie split the commission with another agent so his take would be around nine grand. An extravagant, tax-deductible meal was well worth it. And it was fun.

Aside from the awkward moments about my age and the unwanted job offer, Lydia and Dwayne were a pleasant enough couple—we'd entertained worse. I thought she was more interesting than he was. He seemed full of himself, though I could be wrong. Maybe he just made a bad first impression.

When the waiter came with dessert menus, Lydia said she couldn't possibly eat another thing. I didn't believe her. A couple of shrimp, a crostini, a salad and a poached piece of fish generally left room for a least for at least two orders of panna cotta. As soon as she declined, Ronnie said, "You know what? We're fine."

The look on Dwayne's face suggested that he'd been dying to enjoy at least one of the eight-dollar desserts while his wife watched. I couldn't help myself, I enjoyed his disappointment, though it did mean I missed out on La Bohème's scrumptious tiramisu.

The bill was settled, the waiter smiled profusely at us. We clamored out onto the sidewalk—no one was drunk exactly, but they were also not sober. Ronnie turned on the professional charm.

"It was so nice working with you both. I hope you love your darling house right up until it's time for me to help you find another one. And if you know anyone who needs an agent—well, I've already given you scads of business cards."

"Oh! That reminds me," Lydia said. She opened the tiny clutch she carried and took out one of her own business cards. I thought she was going to give it to Ronnie—though I was sure he had all her information—instead she held it out to me. "I've got time to see you on Friday around lunch. I mean, if you change your mind—It's a terrible job, but we're trying to do good things. And we really could use the help. The address is on the card. Just come by."

It had been an unseasonably hot day, reaching almost eighty-five; now the temperature had fallen, and was hovering below seventy. It was the kind of California weather that made you carry a coat and then forget it wherever you went. When you needed it—and eventually you did—it would be in the car or at a friend's or at that taco place where you'd had lunch.

After they left, Ronnie and I walked out to Ocean where I'd parked. I drove a 1994 Jeep Wrangler, five-speed, forest green with a beige hard top. I loved it. Some days more than my boyfriend.

After we climbed in, I said, "Why did you tell her I used to be a police detective? You know I was lying when I told you that."

"When she told me she needed an investigator, I thought you might want to do it. So, I told her you'd been a cop. And I didn't know you were lying. I believed you. I still do."

"I'm sure I was drunk when I said it."

"All the more reason to believe you."

"Ronnie, you know what guys are like. You shouldn't believe a word for the first six months."

He looked unhappy for a moment. That tore at my heart, so I started the Jeep. I was about to pull out when he said, "Most guys lie at the beginning. But not you. I think that's when you told me the truth."

"So, I'm a liar now."

He shrugged.

"If I'm such a liar, why are we still together?"

"Because, I think someday you'll tell me the truth."

TWO

February 9, 1996
Tết, Year of the Rat
Friday

These are the things I tell people about myself: I was born in February of 1954. I grew up in the Detroit area. I went to U of M for two years, well, three semesters. I was in the Marines for four years. In the eighties, I was married to a woman and managed a Denny's in North Hollywood. Most of the time I was married I had sex with men. Okay, all of the time. After my divorce I went through a bad patch, bartending in a couple of different bars in Silverlake. Then I met Ronnie Chen and he pulled me out of my slump. The only part that's true is the part about meeting Ronnie.

I have at hand a number of things to say when people get too nosey. If I run into someone from Detroit, I say that my family moved around a lot and imply that we were constantly being evicted. No one wants to talk about your childhood of poverty. If I encounter a U of M classmate, I talk about how few classes I went to and how much drinking I did and how I was tossed out for being such a bad student. The Marines, well, I don't know very much about them so all I ever say about the Marines is that I worked in intelligence as an aide to a general I'm forbidden to name. I really can't talk about the work I did there. It was top secret, after all.

People are often familiar with the Denny's I claim to have worked at, but I've never meet anyone who knows anyone who ever worked there. And no one asks questions about my pretend wife. Her pain is too embarrassing to talk about. Sometimes even I feel bad about what I did to her. I've been lying about myself for a long time. It's become a habit. Or maybe an addiction.

The Freedom Agenda was located in a single-story storefront, in between an art supply store and a struggling record store. There was a gay bookstore in the neighborhood somewhere, I knew that because I'd been once. I also knew the store was going to die because the neighborhood was a sort of no man's land: no crowds, very little foot traffic. The rents were the cheapest you could get in Long Beach and there were a lot of Section 8 apartments nearby. Not the sort who frequent gay bookstores. Since it was clearly on its way out, I wondered if I should drive around until I found it again and go there instead of The Freedom Agenda. It would certainly make more sense.

Even though the job had stayed on my mind for two days, up to the point when I got into my Jeep and pointed it toward downtown, I didn't believe I was going to meet Lydia Gonsalez again. At least, not about a job. But there I was parked across the street from her office. Most of me was ready to get out and cross the street. My stomach, however, was ready to jump out of my body and run away screaming. I took a few deep breaths and a Tums to calm it.

All right, yeah, I had some experience. Maybe I was an investigator of sorts. A long time ago. Maybe I'd even liked it. It can be satisfying to work out answers to truly difficult questions—and murder is always a difficult question. It was also a terrible burden to look at the kind of things people did to each other. To know how easy it was to slip over the line and find yourself every bit as horrible as the people you investigated. Did I want to go back to that? No.

But maybe this would be different. Lydia's clients were innocent. I assumed she would drop them if they weren't. That was an interesting idea, walking away if you discover your client really *is* a homicidal maniac. Not that I didn't believe even the guilty deserved a skillful and committed defense. I just didn't see any reason why I had to be party to it. I liked the idea of righting wrongs much more than protecting the guilty from the abuses of the system. I put it down to having seen too many Disney cartoons when I was a child.

Finally, I got out of the Jeep and crossed the street. I walked into the office and a bell rang over my head, like I was walking into an old-time grocery store. Come to think of it, the building might have been exactly that at one point. I was in a kind of lobby where there were several wooden chairs, a wide desk and a pretty black girl sitting behind a computer. She looked over the monitor and asked, "Do you have an appointment?"

"Sort of. Lydia told me to come by."

"Just come by? There was no Friday attached to that?"

"Yeah, I guess there was." I shrugged. "Around lunchtime."

Scowling, the girl picked up the phone and her finger hovered over an intercom button. "Can I tell her who's here? Or is that a little fuzzy too."

"Dom Reilly."

She pressed the button, but before it rang Lydia came out of the office behind her. It was really too small an office space for an intercom system. You could hear everything through the walls.

"Dom! Come on back," she said. She was chewing and had two napkins in her hands. Today she wore tailored slacks with heels and a loose white top. It was more flattering than the outfit she'd worn to La Bohéme but not by much.

She led me to her office, which was the second one down a narrow hall. Beyond the two offices was a large open space filled with a few chairs, several folding banquet-sized tables and a lot of cardboard boxes. Lydia's office had a built-in bookcase on one wall. It was crammed from edge to edge with law books. She noticed me looking at it.

"I don't know why I bother. They're all on CD-ROM now. It's just that I paid for them so I feel like I should show them off. Sit, sit."

I sat in a leather chair across from her smallish wooden desk. It felt like a starter desk. One that would go by the wayside when she moved up to bigger cases, bigger offices, a bigger life. There was an aura around her that said that's exactly what would happen.

On her desk were two Styrofoam clamshell containers. One was open and I saw that there were still two tacos, rice and beans inside. She picked up the other container and offered it to me.

"Chicken molé tacos. Amazing."

"You bought me lunch? You didn't know I was coming."

"I had a pretty good feeling."

"Why? I didn't say anything remotely encouraging?"

"You took my card."

"I could have thrown it away."

"Then I'd have two lunches."

Smiling, she took a bite of one of the tacos. She waved a hand at me that told me I should start eating. I opened the container and took out a taco. As I bit into it, Lydia moved a couple of fresh napkins to the front of her desk for me.

I hadn't exactly dressed for an interview. I was in 501s, Vans and a black canvas shirt with a white undershirt underneath. I knew, from having taken a good look at myself that morning, that my salt-and-pepper hair needed a cut and I could probably use a nose job. My nose had been broken a couple of times in different bar fights and now looked like a deformed mushroom in the middle of my face. If I was more comfortable with surgery, I might get it fixed. It would be nice to breathe through it again. I looked a lot like what I was—a part-time bartender at a dive gay bar.

When she finished her second taco, Lydia took a break and started. "So, tell me about your work experience."

"I spent about ten years managing a Denny's in Hollywood. Then I catered for a few years before I started bartending."

"And you were in the military?"

"Marines."

"Tell me about that."

"I can't. It's classified."

"Intelligence. So, you do have some skills."

"Not really. Mostly typing. On a typewriter."

"I see. Did you bring a resume?"

"No. Sorry."

She was going to throw me out in a minute and that was fine. I could tell Ronnie I'd tried, and life would go back to what it was. Safe, predictable, manageable. I would be relieved. Eventually, I would be—

"It's part-time," she said, making her decision. "I know you have another job so we can work around that. It's fifteen an hour. Pathetic, I know. If things go well, I may be able to raise that. If they don't, we can consider a suicide pact."

"Wait, you're hiring me?"

Ignoring that, she took a bite of her third taco. The look on her face was straight out of a porno. When she was finished chewing, she closed the clamshell without finishing that last taco and said, "A licensed PI is thirty bucks an hour—if I get lucky and he's kind of shitty. The fifteen I'm paying you will be taxed. I can't pay you under the table, so don't ask. You'll be an employee just like my secretary, sorry, assistant. No paid sick days, no vacation days, no 401K. Am I making this sound appealing enough?"

"I really don't think I want the job." I knew that's what I should say so I said it.

"You showed up."

"I have a demanding boyfriend." Actually, he hadn't mentioned the job since the dinner.

She smiled at my comment, then said, "There's another lawyer, Edwin Karpinski. He works mainly out of an office in downtown L.A., but he does show up from time to time. His main function is to go to court dates with me. Believe it or not, there are still judges who don't really like women lawyers, especially the religious ones. Every so often, I let Edwin do everything in court while I act like I'm just there to handle the paperwork. I don't particularly enjoy the ruse, but if it's good for the client I'll put up with it."

She took a long draft on a large paper cup filled with pop. That's when I realized she'd gotten one for me and it was sitting on the edge of the desk, so I too took a sip. Root beer. Watery.

"How's the taco?"

"Delicious." I was nearly done with my second one.

"Aren't they? Little place on Broadway. Sleazy but oh-my-God the food."

She glanced at the closed clamshell as though she might open it and finish her last taco. But then she went back into her spiel. "We also have a paralegal who works part-time. Well, less than part-time. There's not much for her to do unless we're about to go into court. We're still ramping up, so that's not happening all that often. Karen made a copy of the file I'm working on right now." She tapped it with a well-manicured finger. "Take it with you, read it. If it interests, you come back on Monday."

She pushed forward a file that was about three inches thick. "If you like what you see there are two more files just as thick and a box full of miscellanea."

"You don't want to tell me about it?"

"I want you to read the file."

"Oh, I will. But I also want you to tell me about it."

I was still hoping I'd talk myself into ditching the job, but if I didn't, I wanted her to tell me about the case because then I'd know what was important to her about it. Even if she stuck to the barest of facts, she'd be telling me a lot about what she thought.

"His name is Danny Osborne," she began. "In 1985, when he was seventeen, he was convicted of raping, torturing and murdering a teenage girl named Audrey Gunderson. The two of them lived near each other in Westmoreland, right over the border into Orange county. Danny lived with his older brother, Duncan, who dealt crack cocaine. Danny was addicted to crack. Presumably, he was helping Duncan out to support his habit. One March day, Audrey's body was found in a drainage canal near Beach Boulevard. They found half a dozen pubic hairs, as well as evidence that she'd been beaten, burned with cigarettes, and had foreign objects inserted inside of her. There was also cocaine in her system, which led the Westmoreland police to Danny and his brother. They interrogated Danny. He confessed."

She stopped. I sat there for a moment.

"I'm waiting for the part where you tell me he's innocent."

"That's in the file."

"But he confessed."

"I suspect you know enough about the police to understand how that happens," she said, making me uncomfortable. She didn't seem to believe me any more than Ronnie did. And she barely knew me. I needed to be a better liar.

"Was he offered a plea deal?" I asked.

"Yes. His counsel was very interested in his taking it."

"But he didn't."

"No."

"So, he recanted?"

"Yes."

I stood up. "Is there a video tape of the confession?"

She reached into a drawer and took out a video, setting it on the corner of her desk within my reach. I took it.

———

Sitting across the street in my Jeep, I began reading the file. It was around one, one-thirty. I didn't have to be at The Hawk until six. The file had been setup backwards with the most recent documents on top.

First was a letter from Chief Assistant District Attorney Vance Piper. The letterhead looked very important. There was a lot of boilerplate language that didn't mean much. The most important sentence was, "We have reviewed the evidence you've provided and don't find it compelling enough to prove Mr. Osborne's innocence. We will oppose any filing you make for a new trial."

Next was the Supplemental DNA report. The most important part of that document read:

1. The results eliminate D. Osborne (item #15-R4) as the source of the DNA profiles from items #2-1R4 and #2-IR5 (pubic hairs).
2. The DNA profiles from items #2-IR4 and #2-IR5 were searched against the California CODIS on November 13, 1995. No match were found.

I wasn't sure I understood it. Was it telling me that both samples had the same DNA and that it didn't match anything in the database? Or was it saying there were two unique DNA profiles? Meaning that there were two rapists rather than one and that neither of them was Danny Osborne?

Why was this not compelling enough evidence for Vance Piper? What more did he want? He couldn't connect Danny to the victim's rape. Presumably that meant he couldn't connect Danny to the murder, right? Or was he planning to say Danny came along and killed Audrey after she was—

Well, Danny *had* confessed. That apparently trumped DNA. Maybe they reasoned Danny raped Audrey without leaving any hairs. *Was that likely?* Honestly, in all the times I'd had sex I never remembered thinking,

Oh, I just left a bunch of hair on him. So maybe it *was* possible to rape someone and not leave that kind of evidence.

But then who was this other guy? Or other two guys? And how could that be explained away? Danny could have had accomplices he'd never mentioned. But why wouldn't he? Why keep them a secret?

Or Audrey could have had a consensual threesome right before she was raped and murdered. I didn't find either of those excuses particularly plausible, so I folded down the corner of the page to remind myself to come back to it.

Next, was a short, snippy letter from Vance Piper agreeing to comply with the motion to release the evidence to the laboratory that did the DNA testing. After that was a letter from a public defender named Colin Waterstone—who very sternly refused to release Danny's file without assurances that Lydia would not be claiming ineffective assistance of counsel. Of course, his reluctance to provide documents that really belonged to Danny made it obvious he had not provided effective counsel.

Next was the actual motion requesting the retesting of the hair evidence. It was nearly ten pages. Behind it was a newspaper article from January 1986. I skimmed it until I found, "…noted criminologist, Jameson Burke, testified that the pubic hairs found on the victim were consistent with defendant, Daniel Osborne, and that there was a high statistical likelihood that the hairs had come from the defendant."

I flipped through quickly, looking for an actual report or transcript of the trial's testimony. There wasn't anything there. Of course, the discovery from the Orange County DA's office would have probably been several boxes—and more than a decade old. And the trial transcript itself, at least a ream of paper. If not two.

At the bottom of the file, I found several important documents. There was a letter from Lydia to the DA requesting access to the trial evidence, specifically the hair evidence and the videotaped confession. She wrote that full discovery would be necessary should DNA evidence prove exculpatory. Behind that was an article from *The Orange County Register* from late May 1985 detailing Danny's arrest and the case against him at the time —information Lydia had already given me.

The final document, or rather the first, was a handwritten letter from Danny Osborne himself. The letter—which had obviously been written out many times—was very neat. It was also full of misspellings and grammatical errors. The script was cursive and looked as though it had been written by a teenager whose handwriting had not yet solidified.

He said that he'd read about The Freedom Agenda in the newspaper and how they used DNA. He wondered if they could get the evidence in his case tested. He said he hoped they'd be able to help him. It wasn't nice in prison.

I closed the file and started the Jeep. Before I could pull away from the curb something in the car chirped. I jumped. My cellular phone was sitting in the console. Ronnie had gotten it for me. Some kind of deal where we got nights and weekends free. Of course, he was the only one who called me, and it was almost never at night or on the weekend.

I picked up the phone, which was the size of a chunky candy bar—the reason it didn't spend much time in my pocket.

"Hello?"

"How did it go?" Ronnie wanted to know.

"I just got out. How did you know I'd come?"

"I just did."

I hated that my behavior was so freaking predictable.

"Did you take the job?"

"I'm deciding. Lydia gave me a file to look over."

"Oh, well that sounds interesting."

"Where are you?"

"I'm in California Heights waiting for a client." California Heights was a neighborhood just north of the 405. "They're late. Did you remember its New Year's?"

It wasn't New Year's New Year, it was Têt. Vietnamese New Year's. Lunar New Year. Also, Chinese New Year. A weeklong holiday.

"My mother is coming to dinner Monday night."

"I remember. What movie are you taking her to see tonight?"

For date night with his mom, Ronnie liked to take her to the movies since, as he pointed out, it was a way to spend time with someone without actually spending time with them.

"I don't know. Maybe *Mr. Holland's Opus*."

"Do you think she'll like it?"

"No. She hates movies."

"She liked *The Joy Luck Club*."

"She wants to have dinner first."

"Uh-oh."

"Exactly."

Dinner was the only reason she agreed to go to the movies with Ronnie. Dinner would inevitably include a nice Chinese girl a few years younger than Ronnie—sometimes second generation, more often newly immigrated and in need of a green card. If Ronnie had the nerve to mention his boyfriend, that meant he'd be going to the movies alone. Consequently, he did his best to always be too busy to make dinner before the movie.

"I've scheduled a new client for five-thirty. That way I'll have to meet her in front of the theat—oh, there's my client. Gotta go. Love you!"

THREE

February 9, 1996
Friday afternoon

The camera must have been in the corner of the room up by the ceiling, because what I was looking at were the tops of two men's heads. The video quality was grainy and poor, and the sound hissed. An orange date stamp in the lower right corner, displaying 4-19-84 THU, took up a lot of space. As did the time code, a row of six numbers: three sets of two with colons between them. The set farthest to the right flipped every tenth of a second.

One of the two men wasn't a man at all; he was a teenager with long, straggly brown hair. The other was middle-aged with a donut-sized balding spot on top of his head that he was probably blissfully unaware of. The balding man sat leaning over a small table with a pad in front of him, while the boy fidgeted in an uncomfortable looking plastic chair shoved into the corner.

"This is Commander Samuel Montero of the Westmoreland Detective Bureau here with Daniel Osborne aged sixteen."

"Danny, Danny, people call me Danny."

"Are you aware you're being taped, Daniel?"

"Yeah, yeah, yeah, the camera's up there." He pointed at the camera and then waved. "Danny, my name is Danny."

"Okay, Danny. Earlier I read you your Miranda rights. I'm going to read them again for the camera. Is that okay?"

"Oh yeah, yeah, sure. It's all right. Go ahead."

Montero slowly read the warning. Danny didn't look like he was paying attention. When he finished the warning, Montero said, "So, you've voluntarily waived your right to have counsel present?"

"Oh—totally. I don't need a lawyer. We're just talking right? Don't need a lawyer to have a conversation."

"That's right, Danny, we're just talking."

"Okay, okay. Fine."

"What's your address, Danny?"

Danny laughed. "Funny question. I don't have an address. So, yeah, that's funny."

"I thought you said you lived with your brother, Duncan."

"Oh yeah, yeah, he uh, well, he threw me out, so I don't live anywhere. You know?"

"That must be tough."

"Huh? Yeah. Ha. Maybe you'll throw me in jail. Then I'll have an address." Danny giggled. It was a strangled sound.

"We've been talking about Audrey Gunderson."

"Audrey? Oh yeah, that's sad. I liked Audrey."

"You said you saw Audrey on the fourteenth. Thursday of last week."

I picked up the remote and paused the tape. 'You said you saw...' That meant this was not the beginning of the interrogation, even though it appeared it might be. *Was that earlier portion videotaped? Or had Montero deliberately kept it off the record? And if so, why?*

I pressed play. Danny was saying, "...said that, I said it. All I really remember is Audrey being at my brother's. I don't know what day it was. A while ago. And she disappeared after that."

"You saw Audrey at your brother's on the fourteenth."

"Okay."

"That's what you told me."

"Okay."

"And you told me much more than that."

"Yeah, I guess I did. Do I have to say that again?"

"Yes, you do."

Danny grew quiet, then asked, "Can I go to the bathroom first?"

The picture jumped, as did the time code. The tape had been edited. From the time code I could see that more than ten minutes had passed. At this point, I had no idea how long the videotaped interrogation was originally. It seemed reasonable that the judge might allow an edited version to be show in court—perhaps with a complete transcript made available to the jury if the defense objected. Although, given Colin Waterstone's protestations it's possible he didn't object.

Montero and Danny were in different positions. Now, Montero was closer to Danny. Almost touching him.

"What happened on the fourteenth, Danny?" He rested a hand on Danny's shoulder.

"I dunno."

"You do know. You already told me. We were standing outside the bathroom."

"Yeah. Okay."

"You'll feel better once you tell me about it. Tell me about the day Audrey disappeared."

"I have to go to the bathroom."

"No, you don't. You have to stay here and talk to me."

"About what?"

"If you keep this up, I'm going to get angry."

Danny stayed quiet. He looked away from Montero at the blank wall. He certainly had the look of someone who'd been caught doing something wrong.

"Um, Audrey was at our place and Duncan had got us some beer—shit, is he in trouble? I can't get him in trouble. He's already mad at me."

"Don't worry about that. Just tell me what you did to Audrey."

"There were these other guys there. I didn't really know them, one guy, Duncan called him Piglet, and the other—

The tape jumped again. Five minutes had passed. I wondered what had happened.

"Are you ready to cooperate, Danny?"

"Yes."

"What time did you and Audrey leave your brother's trailer?"

"Audrey left around four-thirty."

"And where did the two of you go?"

"She didn't leave with me, she left with—"

"Danny, this isn't going to help you unless you tell the truth. You've already told me that you and Audrey left together. You just need to say it for the video."

"I don't know if I meant that. Can I go to the bathroom?"

Another jump. Before anyone said anything, I pressed pause. *What was going on? Why did Danny keep asking to go to the bathroom? Montero mentioned taking him to the bathroom once, was there a reason he kept wanting to go? Was something wrong with his bladder?*

While I was still in my Jeep, what I'd read seemed to suggest there might be two DNA profiles, meaning two men's DNA on Audrey's body. Maybe I was reading it wrong, but Danny claimed, briefly, that the girl left with these two guys, Piglet and someone else. If the DNA *is* from two men, that becomes a compelling statement. Or almost a statement. It's barely on the tape. *Was it cut off deliberately?*

Montero obviously thinks Danny is lying. *Why though? Why does he think that?*

I pressed play and Danny began to speak. "We went to her place. Audrey's family lives right around the cement river. She invited us all. Duncan couldn't come, but P—sorry, I forgot. Just me. It was just me. She invited just me. Um, when we got to Audrey's we went into her bedroom and then I, um, well, I-uh raped her and then I strangled her with her underwear."

"Her bra."

"Right. Sorry. Forgot. Her bra."

"Then what happened?"

"Then she was dead. Yeah, dead."

"Did you do anything to her after she was dead?"

"No. God, no," Danny said, looking disgusted.

"Okay let's skip that for now. How did you get her to the canal?"

I hit pause again. By that point the hair on the back of my neck stood straight up. I'd begun to notice Danny's demeanor. Sometimes he was slouching in his chair, lethargic. And other times, just now, his eyes were bright and his speech rapid.

Danny didn't need to go to the bathroom to pee, he was going there to get high. *Did Montero know? Was he using the trips to the bathroom to get Danny to confess? Was he giving Danny drugs or was he just allowing*

Danny to use what he'd come in with? And did it matter? Montero's knowing at all tainted the confession. Didn't it?

I let the tape continue while I looked through the file. Montero asked, "How did you get her to the place where you dumped her body."

"Oh. Oh, um, it was dark. I put her into the back of her sister's car. It was dark by then."

"Where were Audrey's parents?"

"They worked. She said that when we were at Duncan's."

"Tell me about Audrey's sister's car. What kind is it?"

"I dunno."

"What color?"

"Blue?"

Montero left a pause.

"Green?"

"Good. The car is green. I told you someone saw you park the car by the canal."

"Yeah, you did."

"And it was late."

"It was."

"So, what did you do to Audrey between the time you killed her and the time you dumped her in the canal."

"I don't want to talk about that part."

"You have to tell us, Danny. You'll feel better when you get it all off your chest."

The image shifted. The timecode had jumped again. I ran the tape back and forth. Nearly an hour had passed.

Danny was crying now.

"You feel bad about what you did," Montero suggested.

Danny nodded.

"You did a terrible thing."

Another nod. Then, "What about Dix and Piglet? They're the ones who really—"

"You're making them up."

"No."

"Yes, you are. You know you are."

"Piglet, I think he used to be fat, I think that's why they call him that.

And Dix, I don't know why they call him that, but he's tall and has blue—"

"What are their real names?"

"I don't know."

"Because they're not real." Montero picked up his chair and moved closer to Danny. "Look, it makes sense that you want to blame this on someone else, but you're never going to feel good again if you don't stand up like a man and take the blame—"

"They *were* there."

"Can your brother tell me who they are? Are they friends of your brother's?"

"Not really."

"And they aren't friends of yours?"

He shook his head. "No, I didn't know them."

"Why were there people at your brother's place neither of you knew?"

"I can't tell you that. I'll get in trouble."

"You *are* in trouble, Danny. You're in a lot of trouble."

"What the fuck are you watching?" a voice behind me asked.

I sat up straight on the white shabby chic, slip-covered couch Ronnie just had to have. My living room, which had disappeared while I watched the tape, came back into focus. The faux fireplace, the orange occasional chairs, the sun porch with the wide window seat.

Behind me stood our roommate, John Gallagher. He was thirtysomething, tall and thin, with bristly blond hair. He wore blue scrubs, running shoes and had a hospital ID attached to his breast pocket. I'd been so absorbed in the tape that I hadn't heard him come in even though the front door was only about ten feet away.

"It's a police interrogation." Then I added, "What are you doing awake? You're usually asleep in the afternoon."

"I worked a double. Is there something wrong with soap operas?"

"It's for this job I'm thinking of taking." Trying not to think about what it was like to work a sixteen-hour shift.

"As what?"

"As an investigator."

"So, this is like a how-to?"

"More like a how-not-to. Hey, since you're here, I want your opinion on something." I ran the tape back to the beginning. "So, the cop mentions coming back from the bathroom. But then the kid wants to go again. Later the he's agitated, talking fast."

John shushed me. He watched for a minute or so and then said, "That kid's high as a kite."

"Really? You're sure?"

"I've been a nurse at Long Beach Memorial for ten years. I know a crackhead when I see one."

"That's what I thought too. He's getting high in the bathroom. The detective, Montero, he has to know, right? I mean, this kid's not hiding anything."

"You smoke crack in a glass tube. It's easy to carry around in your pocket. But it smells. A weird sort of artificial, burned-plastic kind of smell. Methamphetamine smells the same way."

"Ah," I said, getting it. There were quite a number of customers who showed up after midnight with a funky smell. Tweakers. "So, the detective knows this kid is high."

"How could he not know?"

I sat there thinking. Montero knew Danny was high while he was being questioned. *The district attorney must have figured it out too, right? What about Danny's attorney? And the jury?* This was something I'd have to ask Lydia about.

I forwarded to the spot where I'd stopped. John sat down at the other end of the sofa.

"—I'll get in trouble."

"You *are* in trouble, Danny. You're in a lot of trouble."

Danny, head hanging, began to sob.

"Just a few more minutes and this will all be over," Montero said kindly.

Danny managed to say, "I want to talk to Duncan."

"You can talk to him later."

"He knows I didn't... do... anything wrong."

"But you did do something wrong. And when you finish telling me about it, this will be over."

Neither of them said anything for a bit. Danny tried to get hold of himself. Then Montero put a hand on Danny's shoulder and rubbed it.

"Don't you want to feel better, Danny?"

"Yeah," he sniffled. "I want to feel better."

"Then tell me what you did to Audrey. After you raped her, after you strangled her, you did something to her."

Danny sighed deeply and then seemed to give up. "I put a bottle into her. And then a broom."

"Those were terrible things to do."

"Uh-huh. Can I go to the bathroom again?"

"No, Danny, let's finish this first."

"And then I can go home?"

"You need to finish telling me what happened and then we'll talk about you going home. What did you do with the bottle and the broom?"

"I put them into Audrey."

"I mean after."

"I left them in Audrey's bedroom."

"No, you didn't."

"I put them in the canal."

"Good. Thank you."

Danny's breathing was heavy enough to hear on the video.

"When you strangled Audrey, what did she do?"

"She died."

"Did she try to fight back?"

"No. Yes. She wiggled a lot, I guess."

"Is that all?"

"She was crying. I felt bad."

"Thank you, Danny."

The taped ended. I looked at John. "So, Danny's doing crack in the bathroom, but he keeps wanting to go back. The drugs aren't working?"

"Crack doesn't last long. Fifteen minutes. Less if you're really addicted or it's not very good quality."

I needed to see the whole interview. It appeared Montero was using crack to extract a confession. If Danny said what Montero wanted to hear then he got a trip to the bathroom.

"And he'll say whatever it takes to get back to the bathroom," I said.

"Yup. That's the way addiction works."

FOUR

February 9, 1996
Friday evening

The Hawk was located on Broadway in a line of gay bars that appeared every few storefronts and was often called The Stroll. It shared space in a long brick building with a much larger, low-end Italian restaurant. Inside, it was little more than a bar, a small space for people to mingle, and two doorless restrooms. Across from the bar was a railing where guys could set their drinks while they stood there. There was a soggy indoor/outdoor carpet, a juke box and a giant metal fan that we turned on when it got too warm. Which was most of the year.

I worked three ten-hour shifts a week—Friday, Saturday, Sunday. I was paid a salary rather than hourly so they didn't have to pay me overtime. That broke down to three hundred a week plus tips. A bad week of tips was four hundred dollars, a good week was six. It was a nice gig.

Friday nights I worked alone with a barback from six to ten. There was a manageable afterwork crowd and then a big bump from ten until two. That's when another bartender came in.

The bar had a reputation as a pickup joint, though I wasn't sure it was well-deserved. There were two kinds of customers at The Hawk: the ones who rarely came and the ones who came every week, maybe once, twice, three times. Those who came in rarely did pick someone up; being a novelty act generally helped. Those who were there all the time thought they came in for sex but willingly settled for alcohol.

Occasionally, the younger ones would disappear into a twelve-step program never to be seen again, while the older ones would just die of heart attacks or liver disease. And sometimes, men of all ages, died of overdoses. And, of course, AIDS was still around. There were new meds—the cocktail. But it didn't save everyone. Some were too far gone.

The Hawk had a beer bust on Sunday afternoons—which I came in early for—and two-for-one long necks on Tuesday nights—which I didn't work unless another bartender was out.

That Friday night around nine it was still quiet. Most of the crowd was still down the street at one of the nicer bars. I stood at the end of the bar furthest from the door, talking with one of our regulars, a woman named Pamela who lived a block away. She was there every night drinking unfathomable amounts of mediocre white wine—only half of which I charged her for. She was close to retirement age and had spent her life doing something with the port that I'd never quite understood.

She was telling me all the reasons she hated Hillary Clinton, which mostly boiled down to the fact that she hadn't restricted herself to picking out new drapes for the Oval Office, when Ronnie popped in and parked himself on the stool next to her. Before he could ask, I made him a Ketel One and cran. For a while, those were called Cape Cods, but along the way people found it too hard to say they wanted a Cape Cod with Ketel One and shortened the whole thing. An extra word or two can mean a lot when you're waiting for a drink.

"How was the movie?"

"Ugh! I hated it. It's about this guy who wants to be a composer and ends up a high school teacher instead. And he accepts it! It's one of those movies that tries to convince you that losing is winning."

"There's nothing wrong with being a high school teacher," Pamela said.

"I know there's nothing wrong with being a high school teacher if that's what you set out to be. Wanting to be something else and ending up a high school teacher, that's failing. And if you're going to tell that story it should be a tragedy and not some sentimental, feel-good drama."

"Did your mother like it?"

"Of course not! She doesn't think real men should be teachers *or* musicians." I set his drink in front of him and he sipped it. "She brought a girl with her. Korean, I think. She thought she was being open-minded because the girl wasn't Chinese."

"Your mother doesn't know you're gay?" Pamela asked.

"Oh, she knows. She just won't allow it."

"Does it work that way?"

Ronnie and I said "No" at the same time.

"I didn't think so."

"Anyway, I had to think of something, so when my mother dragged us out for ice cream afterward I explained in extensive detail why Kylie Minogue is the next Madonna. Nothing. Then I found out she loves *The Real World*, so I went on and on about Pedro, the cute Cuban kid who died of AIDS, and then she got it. I won't be seeing her again."

"Doesn't your mom think it's a problem that you own a house with another man?"

"Two houses. And no, she doesn't think it's a problem. She pretends that we're business partners no matter how many times I tell her we're not. My relationship with my mother is like that movie, *Groundhog Day*. I come out to her and then the next day I have to come out to her again and again and again. It's exhausting."

He took a sip of his drink. "Sweetheart, are you mad at me? There's barely any vodka in this drink."

There were at least two shots.

"If you don't like the way I pour go somewhere else."

Pursing his lips at me, he asked, "Did you decide about that job?"

I was probably going to take it since I kept thinking about the file Lydia had given me in between customers. Still, I wasn't sure I wanted to tell him. Not just yet.

"Maybe."

"I knew you'd like it. It'll be good for you. You look happier already, I can tell."

I leaned over the bar and said, "You know they let me drink on the job, right?"

He raised an eyebrow. I wasn't drunk and he knew it. These days I only ever had one drink—if I even had that. I didn't like alcohol as much as I once had. It had betrayed me too many times.

Ronnie turned to Pamela and said, "Dom is going to be the lead investigator for this not-for-profit, The Freedom Agenda. They get innocent people out of prison."

"There aren't a lot of innocent people in prison, are there?"

"Who knows? The guilty ones say they're innocent and the innocent ones say they're innocent. How do you tell them apart? Oh wait, that's where Dom comes in."

I had to wander off and make some drinks for customers in the pickup line. Then I took care of two guys sitting at the far end of the bar. Finally, I went back down to Pamela and Ronnie. She was talking about Hillary Clinton again and Ronnie said, "I like a strong woman."

"Like your mother?" I asked.

"Well, except her." He smiled at me and winked. Honestly, he was probably the only man I'd ever been with who enjoyed being teased. He seemed to thrive on it.

I met Ronnie Chen in front of a sex club on Santa Monica Boulevard called The Meat Rack. It was sometime in the summer of 1992, a few months after the riots. Ronnie knows the exact date and reminds me every year. Technically, I'd met him inside. But you don't really meet in a sex club—and you certainly don't speak. For one thing the techno music was too loud, and for another it wasn't called a conversation club.

That part of Santa Monica Boulevard was not very nice then, and probably still isn't, with a lot of warehouses and industrial buildings doing who knows what in the daytime. The wise thing to do was walk to and from your car as quickly as possible. Which was exactly what I was trying to do when I left the club. I was halfway to my car when the very cute, very young part-Asian boy I'd just dallied with came up behind me.

"Hey, what's your name?"

I was a bit taken aback. I turned and stared at him long enough that he asked, "You do know your name, don't you?"

"The question is why do *you* want to know my name?"

"Why shouldn't I want to know your name?"

Fearing we might go on like that until dawn, I told him my name. "Dom. It's Dom."

"Like in dominate? I bet that makes you popular."

"Like in Dominick."

"My name's Ronnie Chen. Can we have dinner some time?"

I stared at him. "So—did you come to a sex club to find a boyfriend?"

"Is that weird?"

"Very."

"Why? I like the way you look, and I liked the little bit of sex we just had."

He called it 'a little bit' because in a sex club there's no place to keep your clothes and there are no private rooms with beds, so in general guys do things they're comfortable doing with their pants down around their ankles and in public—granted, some guys are much, much more comfortable than others, but it does tend to restrict a lot of the crowd.

Ronnie continued, "Now I want to talk to you and see if I like that too."

"And if you like talking to me?"

"Maybe wedding bells. Or rather commitment ceremony bells. Would you like to have a commitment ceremony some day?"

"It's a bit early for a proposal."

"Is it?"

"You come on very strong."

"Compliment or criticism?"

"Both." I looked him up and down. He was kind of adorable in his white Polo shirt and pink linen shorts. It had been over a hundred degrees that day and at four in the morning it was still well over eighty. "I don't want to have dinner. How about breakfast? Now."

"Sure, that'll work."

I was driving a Toyota MR2 from the '80s at the time, a car that was much too small for me. When we got into the two-seater, Ronnie said, "Wow, it's a good thing we already had sex. We sure couldn't do it in here."

Then we drove around looking for a 24-hour restaurant. After about five minutes, Ronnie said, "You're not from L.A., are you?"

"Why do you say that?"

"Because all the 24-hour places are on the West Side."

As it turns out, he was right, so we ended up buying coffee and stale donuts at a 7/11 and eating in the car. With powdered sugar on his lower lip, Ronnie launched into a long explanation of his family history. On one side, his family had been in California for five generations, dating back to the Chinese immigration influx to work on the railroad. Even though there weren't a lot of Chinese women in California at the time—and it was illegal for a Chinaman to marry anyone else—his great-great-grandfather managed to find one. After that though, his relatives weren't quite so picky—and the laws loosened up—so they started marrying Irish women, Swedish women, Native American women. By the time Ronnie's father was born—other than their name—the family wasn't very Chinese.

"Then, my father went into the Army and got sent to Vietnam, where he met and married my mother."

"So, your mother is Vietnamese."

"Don't ever say that to her. She's Hoa, which is a Chinese minority in Vietnam. They still speak Cantonese, and up until the fall of Saigon ran just about everything. Not that it matters. My mother came here in the sixties, and now she tries to pretend she's Chinese because she thinks Americans respect the Chinese more than Vietnamese."

"And what do you think?"

"To most Americans we're all just zipperheads."

"That's not a very nice word."

"I know, it's not is it? You're Irish, I suppose?"

"Mostly."

"I'd call you a Mick but that's really lame. This coffee is disgusting by the way."

"It's like drinking tar."

"The stale donut makes up for it though. So where are you from?"

"Back East."

"Back East where?"

"Back East."

"Ah, a man of mystery."

"You know, if you want to find people to talk to you could just go to a bar."

"I don't like alcoholics."

"I'm a bartender. And I like to drink." Well, at the time I did. It was later that I started thinking it was a bad idea.

"Do you shake at ten o'clock in the morning?"

"Rarely."

"Wonderful. You've passed. Where do you bartend?"

"The Gauntlet."

"I've been in there. Does that mean you're into leather?"

"It means I'm into paying my rent. Did you meet anyone when you came in?"

He shook his head. "Silly me, I should have talked to the bartender."

"You realize I'm much older than you are."

"I hate having sex with guys my age. They don't know what they're doing."

"I doubt that's true. I've had some very good sex with people your age. Even when I was your age."

"Maybe it's a generational thing then. You're a baby boomer, aren't you?"

"I suppose."

"They're calling my generation Generation X."

"I've never heard that before."

"It sounds dirty, so I'm sure it will catch on."

We kept talking. He wanted to know my dreams, but I told him I'd run out of them, so he told me his. He'd just gotten his real estate license and wanted to amass a property empire.

"You want to be a slumlord?"

"Of course not. It's a hassle to raise poor people's rent. I want to rent to rich people who won't mind the rent I charge. Do you want to own property?"

"Do you want to be my real estate agent?"

"Among other things."

The whole thing was outrageous. He didn't know me. And I was sure he wouldn't still be in my car if he did. I decided the best thing to do was be honest enough that he'd go away.

"I killed a man once. A long time ago."

"Just one?"

That made me laugh. It was not a normal response. "Yes, just one."

"I'm guessing he deserved it."

"He did. But it's not my place—"

"You're going to have to try harder than that to get rid of me."

I was staring at him. He really did have a nice face. Wide cheeks, dark eyes that sparkled in the light that came from the convenience store, silky black hair, nice lips, dimples even.

Then someone was banging on the window. I turned around and there was the guy who'd sold us the God-awful coffee and the horrible donuts. Screaming at us.

"You cannot sit here! Go away!"

I started the car and pulled out of the lot.

"Where can I drop you?" I asked Ronnie.

"Where do you live?"

"I live in Silver Lake. But that wasn't the question—"

"You can drop me at Silver Lake."

In other words, he was coming home with me. I was too tired to fight it. It wasn't far, so we arrived pretty quickly. The sun was about to come up. He'd chattered the whole way, talking about music he liked, TV shows, I don't remember what else. By that time, I was desperate for sleep.

The building I lived in then was from the forties, a long narrow building with about fifteen single apartments on each of its three floors and a hundred layers of paint. My apartment was on the second floor with a nice calming view of the brick wall next door.

Once inside, Ronnie took it all in. Not that there was much to take in. A mattress in the middle of the floor, a portable TV, a stack of books— mostly mysteries, I'm embarrassed to say. Some gay porn magazines.

Under his breath he said, "Thank God. I've arrived just in time."

FIVE

February 12, 1996
Monday morning

Muck. Brown muck at the bottom of a pond. My face pushed into it. Hand on the back of my head, holding me down. I'm struggling. Needing to breathe. Water icy. I flip over, away from the hand, flailing. My shirt is grabbed. I'm pushed back into the muck. Must breathe. I try to strike my attacker, but the water slows my blow to harmless. I clutch him. Pull him tight. I'll take him with me. We'll drown together. He slips away. Rises out of the water. Moonlight catches his face. My face. Me.

I woke up and chuckled. My subconscious was ham-handed. I dreamed I was drowning myself and that was silly. I was a happily partnered, middle-aged man with a lucrative part-time job about to start a more interesting and possibly important part-time job. I was not, metaphorically or otherwise, drowning myself. Life was good and had been good for a long time.

Ronnie had already gone to his office. As a real estate agent, he could certainly sleep in on a Monday morning if he wanted to. His clients needed him mostly in the afternoon and evening. And sometimes he did sleep in, but most of the time he was down at his office checking the MLS for new listings and recent sales, doing follow up calls from his showings over the weekend, responding to any offers or counteroffers which might have come in.

As I sat at the counter in the kitchen eating a pile of scrambled eggs, John came in the back door, his shift at Long Beach Memorial having ended. Memorial was the hospital that treated many of the city's indigent, so the hospital was always over-crowded and John was always busy.

"Rough night?" I asked when I saw him.

He just shrugged and went over to the Mr. Coffee and poured himself some coffee. "I keep thinking about that videotape you showed me."

"Me too."

"Why would the police want someone to confess to something they didn't do? I mean, they're either protecting someone or just plain lazy."

I shook my head. "Righteous. They believe they've got the right guy; they feel it in their gut. So they make the pieces fit."

"Gut feelings? Like on TV shows?"

"Exactly. Cop shows are probably the worst thing to ever happen to policing."

"Yeah, *E.R.* makes it look like we resuscitate people eighty percent of the time."

"You don't?"

He shook his head. "More like twenty, if that. The newbies are really depressed by that. They thought they'd be saving lives right and left, not helping people die."

"Someone has to," I said, glumly.

"Hey, did you find another roommate, yet?"

Typically, we had two roommates. Our last roommate, a twentysomething named Brad, had found the love of his life and moved out right after Christmas.

"We're still looking," I told John. And we were. We were just kind of picky. We preferred flight attendants. Typically, they were gone half the month or more. Brad had worked for Delta out of Long Beach Airport. He'd promised to put up a notice in the employee lounge but may have been distracted by his oh-so romantic life.

If we couldn't find a flight attendant. We liked people like John who worked nights and did around twenty hours of overtime in a week. We preferred the money every month to the actual human beings. I did like

John as it turned out, but that was hardly a given when you entered into these things.

"I'll ask around at work," he said, then rolled his eyes. "I have got to get to bed."

"And I have to get to work."

————

"Thank God, you're here," Lydia said when I walked into the Freedom Agenda offices on Monday morning. She was standing next to Karen's desk with a jelly donut in one hand, trying to eat it without getting any powdered sugar onto her tailored, navy blue suit. "I was pretty sure you'd show up, but I was afraid of jinxing it."

"The file is pretty interesting. I have a lot of questions."

"Good, I was hoping you would. I have a pretty full morning. Conference call with Edwin and then I have to, have to, *have* to write a motion for another case we're working on. I should be able to sit down with you around eleven-thirty. Until then, I'm going to have Karen show you our files, which I want you to start reading. She'll explain. This is just something you can do in-between other assignments."

"Okay," I said dubiously. Had I just signed up to do their filing? That was not going to thrill me.

"Good. I'll talk to you in a couple of hours." And then she hurried off to her office.

Karen looked at me and rolled her eyes. "Come on. Time to throw you to the wolves."

I followed her back to the large room that sat behind the two offices. We went directly to the banquet tables I'd seen before. What I hadn't noticed was that there was some kind of system of numbered trays on one of the tables. The trays were labeled 0-5, but only trays 0 and 1 had files. Each had lots of files, with tray 1 having the larger stack.

Karen stood by the table and took a deep breath. "So, Lydia got Jimmy Claxton released right before Christmas and it was in a lot of newspapers. Mostly just California but still a lot. Which is good cause we got some donations but not so good because we got a lot more letters from prisoners who want Lydia to get them out. I guess they get a lot of newspaper subscriptions in prison. So we gotta deal with all these letters."

That's when she pointed to half a dozen boxes scattered on the floor, which seemed to be full of letters that had not yet been dealt with. My mouth may have dropped open.

"A lot of the letters, they say, 'Hey, this is my name, get me out.' I write back to them and say, 'We can't get you out unless you send us a whole lot more information' and this other part that Lydia wrote which tells them they better be innocent or we're gonna drop them like a hot potato. I mean, she doesn't say it like that. She says it in lawyer-speak, but they know if they're guilty they're just wasting their time."

"They've got time to waste."

"Oh, I don't think it's gonna stop the guilty ones either, but Lydia's got to try." She took another deep breath. "Anyway, we've been trying to come up with a system to weed out the guilty ones. This is what we have so far. If we get a letter with enough information to start, I go onto Lexis/Nexis and try to get information about their cases. Newspaper articles and stuff. There's usually not much. I spend at least one day a week in downtown LA at the big library. Basically, I find out whatever I can without spending much money. Are you following me?"

"Um, yeah."

"Good. Once I've gotten some basic information, I read everything. If there's any mention of anything that can be tested for DNA—blood, saliva, hair, fingernails, spunk. You're gonna get real tired of talking about spunk in this job, by the way. If there is spunk, then I give the file a 1."

She picked up a file from Tray 1 and showed me that there was a sign-off sheet stapled to the file. The top initials were KA—Karen's I assumed—and she'd written the number 1 next to them. Below them were the initials DR, LG and EC.

"When did you do all this?"

"I started Thursday. Lydia was pretty sure you'd take the job."

"I guess so."

"Anyway, if there's nothing to test the file gets a zero. So what you're going to do is, you're going to read *all* the files, the zeroes and the ones, and give each one a score between 2 and 4. You're looking for other things that would help exonerate our potential client. Things like ineffective counsel, witnesses who perjure themselves, confessions that might be a problem, anything exculpatory that might have been missed."

"That's going to be kind of hard with a just a newspaper article or two to look at."

"Don't worry, you don't have to be right. Lydia wants you to use your gut." She gave that a little roll of her eyes. "If you think there's anything to work with give the file a 4. If you don't, give it a 2. If you're on the fence, that's a three. Got it?"

"Then what happens?"

"Put the number next to your initials and then add the file up, and it goes in the corresponding tray. So, if I give a file a 1 and you give it a 4 then that's a 5. So, Lydia wants to read the 5's first. If she's interested, we'll request the trial transcripts."

"And then she's going to read them?"

"No, that's probably going to be you and me."

"Oh. Why don't we just have whatever evidence there is tested for DNA?"

"Because it costs a fortune and we have to pay for it."

That was a great explanation.

"Got it."

"So, go ahead and jump in. If you have any questions, I'm right up front." She started to walk away but stopped, "Oh, I forgot the most important part. The coffee machine is right over there. If you finish the pot, make another."

Then she did walk away, leaving me there alone. She'd said she was throwing me to the wolves, but these wolves were sleepy and mind-numbing. This wasn't what I'd signed up for. Really, it looked like it might be one of the most boring jobs I'd ever had. Yes, I'd had jobs where I dealt with mountains of paperwork, but this job looked particularly depressing. Is this really what I wanted to do? I was nearly fifty, shouldn't I be doing more with my life than quantifying desperation?

I didn't know how to answer that question, so I went over to the coffee machine—which was on yet another banquet table next to a small refrigerator—and poured myself a cup. Ignoring the powdered creamer and fake sugars, I took a sip. It was bold and intense, with undertones of stale ashtrays and motor oil. But it was free, so I drank it.

I sat down on one of those beige metal folding chairs people keep in their closets for parties and wakes. It took maybe five minutes before it became incredibly uncomfortable. Taking the top five files off the stack in tray 1, I read through them quickly not bothering to score them. I wanted to get a sense of what I was dealing with before I started giving out scores.

Karen was right. These guys—and they all seemed to be guys—had much more to say than just get me out. The ones I'd been given knew their cases inside out. They weren't shy about calling witnesses liars, they swore on stacks and stacks of bibles that the DNA would show they were innocent. Each of the letters was two or three pages long, handwritten in tightly lined prose—just like Danny's—as though paper was scarce and they couldn't waste it. In fact, that might be true. I had no idea how hard it was to get paper in prison.

I really couldn't tell if they were truly innocent or simply bright psychopaths. One guy noted that he'd never been arrested before being arrested for rape and murder. I gave him a four. It seemed unusual that he'd never been arrested. People don't typically begin committing crimes with rape and murder, they work their way up. Along the way, they get caught peeping or fondling or assaulting, or even raping. In fact, murder is often a result of their having been caught before. Murder is destroying the star witness. Murder, in their eyes, is a way to stay out of prison.

Another guy actually took some responsibility saying, 'I may not be such a great guy, but I never done nothing like this." Maybe he was just a really good liar, but I didn't think so. He'd overheard one of the officers saying to another: "We know he's a bad guy, if he didn't do this, he did something else." That was not an uncommon sentiment when you're on the job. It was wrong, of course. Suspicion is not fact and using it as a justification for bad police work makes you one of the bad guys. In the end I gave that guy four points and moved him to the top.

———

About twenty after eleven, Lydia came back, poured herself a cup of coffee, and said, "Come on. I'm ready for you."

Setting aside the file I was reading and grabbing the Danny Osborne file I'd spent the weekend with, I followed Lydia into her office. I'd made a list of my questions and placed them at the front of the file. I took them out and was about to start, but Lydia asked, "How was your weekend?"

"Good. I spent most of it with this file."

"Oh, I hope Ronnie doesn't hate me."

"I don't spend a lot of time with Ronnie on the weekend."

"No?"

"He spends his weekends with people like you, selling them houses."

"Oh, I didn't think of that. I should have, I guess. We spent the weekend packing," she said, answering a question I didn't ask. "Okay, let's start."

"The first question I have is about the Supplemental DNA report. Under point #2 it says, 'No match were found' leaving an odd space between match and were."

Lydia set her coffee down and picked up a file from the side of her desk. It was similar to the one I had on my lap, in that it was thick. It was also similar to two other files it was stacked with. I was pretty sure all three files were Danny Osborne.

She flipped through and reread the letter.

"It's a grammatical error. These lab types aren't always very verbal—" She stopped, reconsidered. "It's the space, that's what bothers you, isn't it?"

"It looks like something was whited-out."

"You think it originally said, 'No *matches* were found.'"

"Yes. Meaning that the hair samples that were sent belonged to two people. Neither of whom were Danny."

"The problem is, I chose the lab."

"Okay," I said, not really seeing the problem.

"The DA's office has the motivation to change the report. But they never handled the report. It came directly from the lab to me."

"Do they ever get their samples done at the same lab?"

"It depends. Normally, they use the state lab in Berkeley. But if there's urgency or a sense of importance they'll use a private lab. But that doesn't always work out. They used a private lab in the Simpson case and there were problems the defense was able to exploit. Most prosecutors are leery of private labs."

Glancing down at the report on my knee, I said, "Okay, so the lab you used is Double Helix, Inc. The technician who performed the test signed it at the bottom: Sylvia Pope. Then it was given a technical review, which is initialed, but I can't read the initials. And then there was an administrative review, also initialed, also unreadable. That means that it could have been changed by either the technical review or the administrative review."

"Well, if there was pressure from the DA—say someone was dangling further work," she speculated, "that would happen at the administrative level."

"So that's where we should start," I said.

"Hold off on that for now," She sipped her coffee. "*If* there is prosecutorial misconduct here, I don't want to tip our hand too soon."

"So, what would the prosecution get out of changing that though? The report is not a match to Danny Osborne. It doesn't really make any difference to his case whether there were one or two rapists."

"That's another reason to wait. We need to figure that out before depositions. I don't like to ask questions I don't know the answers to. Let's move on."

"The confession. It was edited. Do you have the rest of the video?"

She shook her head. "At this point, it was hard enough to get what was used at trial."

"On the tape, Montero says Danny is sixteen. Shouldn't he have had a parent present?"

Shaking her head, she said, "Not in California. In other states, yes."

"The interview began before the tape. Do you know how much time Montero spent with Danny before starting the tape?"

"An hour, maybe."

"That's a long time."

"I agree with you, but Montero testified that when they brought Danny in he wasn't a suspect. He claims he started the tape when Danny began to confess."

"He was high."

"Danny? Yes, I suppose he was. He was a drug addict at the time."

"He was high on crack. Do you know how long a crack high lasts?"

"What is it you're getting at?"

"A crack high lasts fifteen or twenty minutes. The tape stops over and over. Danny was being allowed to go to the bathroom and get high. There's no way Montero didn't know that was happening. Crack has a very particular—"

"It doesn't make any difference," she said.

"What do you mean—"

"I mean legally it doesn't make any difference. A confession is admissible even if the defendant is drunk or high. In fact, a jury might believe the defendant is more likely to be truthful when they're high. They'd certainly believe it was more likely he was a rapist. Drug addicts don't have a great reputation."

"Montero was coercing him by withholding his access to drugs."

"That's implied, certainly, but there's no direct evidence. There are no drugs on the tape. Neither of them speak directly about drugs. There's no real evidence of coercion."

I wanted to fight that, to insist that we should be able to put that in front of the judge and get a new trial, but she knew what she was doing. If she said the confession was admissible then it was.

"What about Dix and Piglet?"

"What about them?"

"Any idea who they are?"

"No."

"No one looked for them?"

"The police didn't."

"And Danny's attorney?"

"I doubt it. He wouldn't have had time."

"Aren't they important?"

"If we get a new trial and we can prove they exist, maybe. But right now there's no corroboration. Danny's own brother claimed they didn't exist when he took the stand."

That surprised me. "He did? Why would he do that?"

"For one thing, maybe they don't exist. For another, Duncan Osborne was a drug dealer. Dix and Piglet would have been there to buy drugs. He wouldn't have wanted to say that on the stand."

"Can we talk to him? Get him to recant?" I asked.

"He died three years ago."

"Overdose?"

"Shot. Execution style in his trailer."

"And they don't know who did it?"

"They probably do know, they just can't prove it."

"Duncan never got caught dealing?"

"He never went to prison for dealing." The way she said that tipped me off.

"You think he was a CI?"

"I do. I think that's why he testified against his brother. I also think he got found out and that's why he got shot. It ticks all the boxes."

I sat quietly. I could probably have thought up some more questions, but I felt like I was striking out left and right. I needed to spend more time watching and listening.

"What's next?" I asked.

"Legally speaking?"

"Yes."

"We're going to file a writ of habeas corpus requesting a new trial. We're going to need to pull together everything, everything that suggests Danny's innocence."

"The DNA isn't enough?"

"No. The DA has made it clear he intends to fight that."

I let that sink in for a moment. "Where do you want to start?"

"Tomorrow I'm driving up to Corcoran to see Danny. Wanna come?"

"Yeah, I do."

"I'll pick you up at eight."

SIX

By the time I got home it was six-fifteen. My head was spinning with all the details from the different files I'd been reading, Danny's case chief among them. Ronnie was in the kitchen cooking, though mainly that meant he was putting things he'd bought on plates. I could tell by the brown paper bag he'd been to Supermarket Saigon in Westmoreland.

He'd already filled a large tray with delicacies: nuts, dried fruits, ginger, coconut chips and dates. It wasn't exactly Vietnamese. He always added things that didn't quite belong, but it was his version of something called Mut Tet. I ate a date, sweet and sticky.

Ronnie came over and kissed me, deeply. I thought he might be trying to get the date back.

"What was that for?"

"How was your first day on the new job?"

"Interesting. When does your mother get here?"

"Ten, fifteen minutes."

"I need to take a quick shower and change. So, what should I expect tonight? Border skirmishes or nuclear war?"

"I don't have the slightest idea what you mean," he lied through his teeth.

I rolled my eyes and went upstairs.

The best way to describe Ronnie's relationship with his mother is to talk about his coming out at age nineteen. It was his first semester in college, and he decided—perhaps foolishly, perhaps not—that he should tell his mother he was gay. When he did, she refused to accept it. She offered to buy him a car if he promised to be straight. Finding that a completely ridiculous and offensive offer, Ronnie accepted. Which is how he ended up with a brand new 1987 Ford Mustang to drive to college. The fact that he'd insisted the car be purple should have been a clue that he was not taking the deal seriously.

Since then, Ronnie has come out to her many times and she always purposely doesn't understand. The first time we met, he introduced me as his partner. She refers to me as her son's business partner, always. Since we owned two houses together—the first, a small two-bedroom over by Wilson High where we lived for a year and a half— it was not entirely inaccurate.

I tried to give their conflict a wide berth. The fact that I'm older than Mai Chen by two years meant that I spotted her points. If I had a child in love with someone my age, I think I'd dislike them as well. Although, certainly Mai Chen disliked me for more than my age. Still, the war was between Ronnie and his mother. If I got hit with shrapnel from time to time, I learned to grin and bear it.

I took my shower in the tiny bathroom off our bedroom. We'd figured out it must have been put in during the fifties. Originally, the one large bathroom on the second floor was supposed to serve all five bedrooms. Well, four. One of the bedrooms was actually what they used to call a sleeping porch. The outside two walls were nothing but windows. In the summer the whole family would sleep in that room in order to catch whatever breezes came along.

Anyway, our bathroom had pink fixtures placed closely together, the tile was gray. I actually liked the little room, though Ronnie kept threatening to rehab it.

When I was done, I came out and got dressed. I picked out a brown corduroy shirt to wear over a nearly new BVD undershirt—it was winter, and we tried not to use the furnace—along with a simple pair of Levi's. I laced up a pair of blue-and-black Vans—I'd still happily be wearing Reebok's, but Ronnie had forbidden me from buying another pair and thrown out all my old ones.

"It's not nineteen eighty-six," he'd said in his most judgmental tone.

Walking out of the bedroom, I heard the sound of the ocean coming from John's room. The door was open, so I peeked in. He was sitting in his underwear at the computer. On the screen was a pier and a view of an ocean. He was playing *Myst*. He'd shown me the game, but I didn't quite get it. Wandering around a virtual environment wondering if something was going to happen seemed pointless since we lived a few blocks from a park and the beach where you could easily wander around wondering if something might happen.

"Get dressed and come down for dinner."

"Do I have to get dressed?"

"Mrs. Chen is coming."

"The dragon lady?"

"Don't call her that."

"Ronnie does."

"He shouldn't. Let's not encourage him."

I went down the stairs. They were interesting—the stairs, I mean. I'd never seen anything quite like them before. At the landing, you could turn left and go down into the living room, or you could turn right and go down into the butler's pantry attached to the kitchen. I turned right.

Mai Chen was already standing in the kitchen wearing a chocolate mink coat and stiletto heels. In her hands was a pink Tupperware box I'd seen on many occasions.

"Hello, Mai, can I take your coat?"

She set the Tupperware on the counter and shimmied out of her coat without so much as looking at me. Underneath, she wore a tailored red dress that showed she still had quite the figure at forty-six.

I stepped into the TV room and hung her coat on a coat rack we had in there – the house didn't have a coat closet anywhere, which was not uncommon in Southern California.

As I came back into the kitchen, I heard Mai ask, "What are you making?"

"I boiled a chicken," Ronnie said. "And I bought a few things at the store. Chung Cake, Gio Cha, and red sticky rice for luck."

"I made Chinese dumplings for the Year of the Rat." She was making it clear that she was celebrating Chinese New Year even if the rest of us were celebrating Tết.

"Thanks, ma, I love your dumplings."

I exhaled. First shots had been fired across the bow with no real injuries.

"Who wants wine?" I asked.

"Me, me, me!" Ronnie said. Then to his mother, "Dom got a new job!"

"Did he? He is not a bartender anymore?" She always managed to make the word bartender sound like it meant syphilitic whore. I handed Ronnie his glass of wine.

"It's an additional job, as an investigator for The Freedom Agenda. They get wrongly convicted people out of prison."

"So, you have two small jobs. I suppose you're too old for one big job."

"You're being rude, ma," Ronnie told her. "You're deliberately misunderstanding things."

"Ronnie, let it be," I said, setting a glass of wine in front of his mother. She hadn't asked, but I knew she'd drink it.

Picking it up, she took a sip. Well, more than a sip.

"You should not speak to me of rudeness. You invite me to dinner and make nothing but Annamese food."

I knew from experience that Annamese was a not very nice word for Vietnamese. Or at least in Mai Chen's vocabulary it was a not very nice word.

"Ma, we're Vietnamese-Americans."

"No. I am Chinese. I was Chinese when I lived in Vietnam, I am Chinese now."

"You've never even been to China."

"Who you are is not where you are."

"Well, I'm Vietnamese-American, emphasis on American."

They'd had this argument before, many times. I never knew who was winning. I went to the fridge and got myself a root beer.

"Mai, how did you like *Mr. Holland's Opus*?" I asked, pouring out my pop.

"Terrible. This is a movie about a bad teacher. He only thinks about himself and what he receives. He does not give good moral guidance to children. Very bad."

John walked in, he wore a polo shirt with a stripe across the chest, a pair of jean shorts and nothing on his feet. I poured him a glass of wine and refilled Ronnie's.

"Hello, Mrs. Chen it's nice to see you."

Knowing she'd probably ignore him, I said, "Tell us about the Year of the Rat, Mai."

"A rat year is a year of wealth and good fortune. Yellow and blue are very lucky colors." With a nasty look at my shirt, "Brown is very unlucky in year of the rat."

"Dom was born in the year of the rat, so this a very lucky year for him," Ronnie said.

"Rat people very unstable. Do not finish what they start."

"What year were you born, John?" Ronnie asked.

"1963."

"Rabbit," Mai said automatically. "Very stubborn."

"Well, I am that."

"I'm year of the monkey," Ronnie said. "Rats and monkeys are the best match."

"For business, yes," Mai conceded.

Afraid Ronnie might object to that, I asked, "Can I start taking things into the dining room?"

"Sure," he said tersely, "the chicken is done."

There was some commotion as John and I began moving things from room to room. Mai gave Ronnie instructions on how to heat up the dumplings, something she did every time she brought them, which was often. So, he knew.

Ten minutes later, I'd opened another bottle of Trader Joe's finest and refilled the wine glasses, while John finished up putting everything on the table. We sat down and began serving ourselves. I asked a question that I knew was somewhat neutral and would take-up about five minutes: "How's business, Mai?"

"Terrible." It always was. "My workers steal from me. I don't know what to do. Mexicans are not honest people."

Thankfully, no one at the table was Mexican.

"Have you thought of installing cameras?" I asked.

"Too expensive. You would bankrupt me."

That was completely untrue. The money was rolling in. She owned three dry cleaners, a minimart in Torrance, and at least one check-cashing place. Her husband had bought her a house in Palos Verdes for eighty thousand dollars during the seventies and then soon after died, leaving her more than enough money to pay off the house and buy the minimart. The house was now worth three quarters of a million. She could afford security cameras.

"I'm sure they're tax deductible."

She made a face that suggested I might have a point but refused to actually utter the words.

"So, Dom, tell us about the work you're doing?" Ronnie asked. He knew a lot about it already; he'd seen the file and we'd talked a little about it the day before.

"Well, this kid was sixteen and a drug addict when he was convicted of raping and murdering a girl. But we tested some hair that was left on the body and it didn't belong to him."

"What about the semen?" John asked.

Mai frowned and cleared her throat. This was not going to be a popular subject.

"You know, I haven't seen a mention of that. I haven't seen an autopsy report yet. I know she was found in a canal though. It might have washed away."

But then why hadn't the pubic hair washed away? I needed to investigate that. I needed to understand it.

"Why are you helping a guilty man?" Mai asked.

"But he's not guilty. That's what the test showed."

"But he is a drug addict. He belongs in prison."

"That wasn't what he was charged with."

"Why does it matter? He is a bad person."

I decided not to argue the point with her. And said, "Well, I guess I'll find out. I'm meeting him tomorrow."

Mai shivered visibly.

"Dom is doing good work," Ronnie said. "Important work."

"Li Na called me."

"I don't know who that is."

"You had dinner with her one month ago. She wants to see you. Have dinner with you. Just you." She smiled, very pleased with herself.

"Ma, you know it's rude to try and fix me up in front of Dom."

Mai did her best to look genuinely confused. "Your business partner will not care if you have wife."

"He's not my business partner."

There was a silence, then Mai said into her dinner, "A wife is very useful thing."

After an uncomfortable pause, John was nice enough to tell us the plot of the latest *X-Files*. After that, conversation drifted to whether aliens existed or not, Area 51, and other conspiracies our government may or may not have carried out. Mai remained relatively quiet for the rest of dinner. She and Ronnie had been locked in their struggle for nearly a decade. I had to admire her stubbornness.

As we got ready for bed that night, Ronnie said, "I don't know how you stand her."

"Your mother? She is who she is."

"I won't ask her here anymore if you don't want."

I took off my undershirt and threw it into the laundry basket. I was looking at a trap. I knew he wanted me to say yes. I knew he wanted me to make the decision for him. But I didn't think it would be good for him if I did—or maybe I didn't want to be the bad guy.

I said, "She's right, you know. A wife would be very useful."

He threw his underwear at me.

SEVEN

February 13, 1996
Tuesday morning

"Do you have a pair of khakis?" Lydia said after rolling down the window of her bronze BMW 5-series.

"What?"

"You're not supposed to wear jeans. I should have told you. And nothing with metal buttons. We're going through metal detectors."

My jeans were 501s so that was doubly a problem. I ran back into the house and put on a pair of khakis, even though they were badly wrinkled, as well as a different pair of Vans, and I changed into a plaid flannel shirt. I grabbed a jean jacket—Corcoran was near Fresno in the central valley which was cooler in the winter and hotter in the summer than L.A. —I'd have to leave it in the car, but it might come in handy.

Five short minutes later, I was climbing into the car. Climbing is perhaps an ambitious word. Folding myself and trying not to grunt too loudly is a better description. Spending a whole day on a metal folding chair was not a good idea at my age.

Though she waited patiently, Lydia didn't ask about my distress. Instead, she said, "We have to make one stop before we leave town," and pulled away from the curb. It was my first time in a BMW 5-series. It was nice enough, but in all honesty reminded me a of a well-appointed Ford Taurus. The lumbar support was a relief, though.

Lydia was dressed in a loose-fitting beige pantsuit and had on a pair of running shoes. Getting in, I'd noticed a pair of matching pumps in the backseat with a low heel.

A couple of turns later and she pulled to a stop in front of The Library, our local gay coffee shop. I got a mocha latte and a chocolate chip muffin; Lydia got a latte with skim milk and a lemon poppyseed muffin. She paid.

Waiting for her change, she asked, "Is this your first time visiting a prison?"

"In California."

As soon as I said that, I regretted it. It didn't exactly fit my bio. *When would I have gone to a prison?* I wondered. As a child in Detroit? While I was supposedly in the Marines? I waited for her to ask what prisons I'd been to before, but she didn't.

She went on, "The trip will take about four hours. We'll be there another two hours—most of that time will be waiting. We'll spend an hour max with Danny, and then we'll come back."

"Long day."

"Why do you think I bought you a muffin?"

Back in the car. She pulled away from the curb, sipped her coffee, and took a CD out of its case. All in rapid succession. At Ximeno she turned north on her way to 7th.

"I hope you like Alanis Morissette. I'm really into *Jagged Little Pill.* It's so addictive."

"That's fine." In general, I would have preferred jazz or classical—or even something from the '80s—but I didn't expect her to have any of that. I asked, "So, you've been to the prison before?"

"Oh yeah, and not just to see Danny. Jimmy Claxton was up at Corcoran as well. It's an easy drive really, we're going to get on the 710 then take it to the 5. It's the 5 most of the way, really."

I sipped my mocha latte and had a pinch of the muffin. I'd grabbed a napkin, so I didn't spread crumbs all over her car. People with expensive cars were usually pretty particular.

"I'm sure you have questions for Danny?"

"Yes, of course. Nothing I've written down, though. I didn't have much time last night, we had Ronnie's mother over for dinner."

"The dragon lady?"

"He really needs to stop calling her that," I said. "There's one thing I wanted to ask *you*. There wasn't any semen on Audrey's body. I mean, I assume that's the case since you're not testing it."

"She was in the canal for approximately seventy-two hours. It would have washed away."

"Why didn't the pubic hair wash away?"

"It was in her mouth."

The mocha latte curdled in my stomach. The crumbs fell off the napkin onto my lap. I broke out in a cold sweat. That was all too easy to imagine. And all too vivid. And all too—

"Are you okay?"

"I am. I'm fine." I croaked, barely able to speak. After a few deep breaths, I added, "I should have thought of that. I just didn't."

"Is that it?"

I inhaled a couple of times before I said, "We need to ask Danny about Dix and Piglet. I need the names of people who might have known them."

She nodded, pulling onto the 405. My father would have said she had a lead foot. It was a little nerve wracking the way she kept changing lanes. She said, "I need someone who can put Dix and Piglet at the Osborne trailer at some point, any point."

"We need to find out who they are," I agreed.

"No, we don't, actually. If we can confirm that they're real people who were floating around at the time, then we can create a theory of another possible killer or killers who the police didn't check out. That's reasonable doubt."

"Wouldn't it be better to find them?"

"That could backfire. If it's not their DNA then we don't have them as possible killers. We need to prove Danny *didn't* do it. We don't have to prove who did. That's up to the police. Our job is to provide enough evidence to overturn the conviction and then create enough doubt that the DA decides not to retry the case."

"Why doesn't Westmoreland have its own DA?"

"It's all Orange County. They have districts. The chief assistant district attorney will decide."

"Vance Piper."

"Yes. He's actually the ADA who prosecuted Danny's case. He's moved up in the world."

"You think that's why he won't accept the DNA evidence? Because it will make him look bad?"

"Possibly. However, some DAs are resisting these cases just on principle. When we get someone out, there's a lot of publicity. Bad publicity in their eyes. Not to mention the monetary settlements."

"You'd think they want justice," I said.

"People want what they think is good for them. If you're the district attorney, you want a case like Danny's postponed until after the next election and then the one after that. There's no real benefit in cooperating."

"There is right and wrong."

She took a sidelong look at me and said, "Don't even pretend to be that naïve."

I sipped my coffee for a few miles. Traffic wasn't bad for early on a Tuesday morning, we were clipping along. The sky was glum.

"What do we do about the brother's testimony?" I asked. "Is there a way to prove Duncan was a CI?"

"That's a nonstarter. If Duncan was or was not a CI, it's not directly related to this case. So it doesn't have to be part of discovery. We could ask a judge to force the prosecution to turn over that information, but he's unlikely to do it. The fact that Duncan may have been a confidential informant doesn't make it more likely that he lied about knowing Dix and Piglet. In fact, in the judge's eyes it could make his testimony more reliable."

"So if we can prove they exist and put them in Duncan's trailer, then we're also proving he lied and his whole testimony is questionable. It also suggests someone put pressure on him to lie."

"Yes," Lydia nodded. "But let's not get ahead of ourselves. We have to prove those boys existed first."

The music was okay, I guess, but halfway through the album Morissette's voice began to sound like fingernails on a blackboard. Lydia began talking again and I tried to focus on her voice instead. "There was study on false confessions done at UCLA three years ago. I have one of the authors of the study, Elizabeth Frickman, set up to talk to Danny in about a week. That's the final piece of what I'm putting together. The DNA evidence, hopefully a witness or two to establish Dix and Piglet existed, and expert testimony on the confession. Those three things should get Danny out and keep him out."

We were quiet for a bit. My mocha latte was suddenly too sweet and already cold. I was tempted to throw it out the window but just held onto it. After we turned onto the 710, I asked, "How's Dwayne?"

"Oh, fine. He thinks he's discovered the next Steven Spielberg, which is his main goal in life. So he's happy."

"And the move?"

"I can't believe we have so much stuff. We've barely made any progress. I have picked out colors for the painters. Well, Dwayne and I picked them out. I had no idea I'd married a man with a grudge against color. Everything he likes is some version of gray."

For some reason that made me ask, "What about Audrey's house—were Danny's fingerprints found there?"

"Only her bedroom was printed. They didn't find anything but claimed that wasn't unusual. You can't get fingerprints off a wool blanket, it's difficult to get prints off sheets. They have to be high-grade cotton and, of course, Audrey's sheets were a low-thread count polyester blend."

"What about the front door? Wouldn't he have had to open it when he left? Shouldn't they have—"

"Yes, they should have. They claim it was an error. There aren't many murders in Westmoreland. Or at least there weren't in the eighties."

"Okay. Did they find fingerprints they couldn't identify?"

"No."

"You said she was beaten before she was strangled. That can be bloody. Did they find her blood in her bedroom?"

"Nothing beyond what you'd normally find in a teenage girl's bedroom. They did try to make something of it though."

"And the bra she was strangled with. Where was that found?"

"It was still around her neck."

"What about cigarettes? You said she was burned. Did they find cigarette butts?"

"They found a lot of cigarette butts, but none that they could connect to the crime. Audrey smoked. So did both her parents."

"Wait a minute, they went through the whole place looking at every cigarette butt there but only fingerprinted the bedroom? Isn't that a problem?"

"One of many."

"Is it possible her bedroom isn't even the crime scene?"

"I'd say that's probable. The reason they've treated it like the crime scene is that it was part of Danny's confession."

After that, we didn't talk much more about the case. Eventually, I asked about her family life. Fourth generation Mexican-American. A sister with a PhD in Chicano Studies from UCLA, brother a medical doctor. She called herself the black sheep since she was the only child who wasn't a Dr. Gonsalez.

"What about you?" she asked. "Brothers, sisters?"

"I'm not close to my family. What did your parents do?"

"My mother is a nurse. My father recently retired from the LAPD."

I thought she might take another stab at asking me for details about my life, but she left it alone. "Is Ronnie's mother as awful as he says?"

"She's not awful; she just does awful things."

"I'm not bad, I'm just drawn that way?" she said, quoting Jessica Rabbit.

"Kind of," I shrugged. "She loves him."

"That doesn't give her a pass."

"No, it's not an excuse. It's more an explanation."

"You like her?"

I couldn't help smiling. "I do, actually."

After that, she didn't say anything for a long time. Eventually, she suggested I try to find a public station so we could listen to the news. It took a while, but I found Valley Public Radio. They were playing classical. Something Russian—which kind of fit our mood.

When we got to the prison, there were two short stone walls on each side of the road. Both had a medallion in the center that said CALIFORNIA STATE PRISON AT CORCORAN on top and DEPARTMENT OF CORRECTIONS on the bottom.

The landscape was flat and sandy. The prison itself seemed to take a cue from the land, with low, wide, dirt-colored buildings, never more than two-stories and spread out. It felt like a giant desert creature resting before devouring its prey.

We stopped at a guard's kiosk, and Lydia told the man who we were and that we were on a list. He pulled out a clipboard and spent nearly a full minute staring at it. It really couldn't be that hard to find two names, could it?

Finally, he nodded and let us pass. We drove down to the large, half-empty parking lot. Once we parked, we put our cellular phones into the glove compartment. I'd already taken off my jean jacket.

"Can I bring a note pad?" I asked.

"Yes."

Not surprisingly, she had a stack of legal pads in the backseat.

"There's a Bic pen in the glove compartment."

I opened the compartment. Underneath our phones there were a half dozen clear Bic pens held together by a rubber band.

"Just take one. More than that and they get testy."

"Does it have to be a Bic?" I asked. It seemed odd that she had six cheap pens in the glove compartment.

"It has to be see-through. You can smuggle things in otherwise."

"Not very big things."

"No, not very big things. Money, pills, nails. With enough patience you can curl a razor blade, I'm told. I've never done it myself."

As I sat there with my mouth open, she got out of the car. Then she opened the back door, slipped off her running shoes, and stepped into her heels. I climbed out as she put her purse on the front seat, shut doors, and then clicked a button on her key chain. The car beeped at her, and it was locked.

We walked toward the visitor's entrance.

"This is a high security prison," she explained. "Charlie Manson is here, Sirhan Sirhan. Many of the inmates live in secured housing, which is one step up from solitary. Danny's in general population. He's not high profile, he's not a gang member, he hasn't been violent since he's been incarcerated. Well, ever, really."

The building in front of us was small with a set of glass double doors. We walked through and were immediately led through a metal detector. Of course, it went off. I explained that I was riddled with surgical screws—so old they were probably rusting. They didn't take my word for it. First, they used a wand, then they frisked me, then I had to allow them to pull up the back of my shirt so they could see the scar on my back.

Finally, we were allowed to go over to reception and sign in. Lydia told the guard we were there to see Danny Osborne. Then she took our keys, our wallets, and the money in my pocket—thirty-five dollars and forty-seven cents. I really hoped I'd get it all back.

The guard explained, "When the buzzer buzzes the doors in front of you will unlock. Proceed through them and then wait. Once these doors lock, you'll hear another buzzer and the second set of doors will open. That will put you into the visitor's room. You'll have the room to yourselves for an hour."

In a low voice, Lydia said to me, "Ronnie told me you were shot once."

"Yeah, well, it's a better story than falling off a bar stool."

"You fell off a bar stool and ended up with screws in your back?"

In my most insincere voice, I said, "Oh, no. I got shot by a bad guy."

The door buzzed in front of us. We followed our instructions and found ourselves in a room that was about thirty feet by forty feet. Scattered around were six tables, each with three seats, all bolted to the floor. I couldn't help but flash on the family dramas that had resulted in the decision to bolt furniture to the floor.

We sat down and waited. Lydia leaned into me and said, "Don't say anything about the case until Danny gets in here."

"You think they're listening? That's not legal."

"No, it's not. Doesn't mean they're not doing it."

After that we didn't say much of anything for about twenty minutes. I thought Lydia might try to find out more about my surgical screws. I knew she didn't believe that I fell off a bar stool. I was surprised her curiosity didn't get the better of her.

Finally, the door on the other side of the room opened and a young man wearing light blue scrubs over a white T-shirt and jeans walked in. Behind him, just on the other side of the door, stood a very large, imposing guard.

Danny's hair was short. He'd shaved that morning—nicking himself once on the upper lip—and had spent a lot of time combing his short brown hair. It was his eyes that got me: cautious, furtive, fearful. He had the look of a stray animal abandoned on the street.

"Hello, Danny," Lydia said. "Good to see you."

"Hi."

As he sat down, she said, "This is Dominick, he's my investigator. I wanted him to meet you."

"Okay."

"It's nice to meet you, Danny. How are you?"

"I'm fine."

Lydia continued, "Danny, do you remember me telling you about the petition I'm filing with the court?"

"Habeas corpus," he said, surprising me at first, but then I remembered where he was. Discussions of habeas corpus were probably as common as homemade tattoos.

"Good," she said. "We have questions we need to ask that will help me put together the petition."

She looked over at me.

"Do you mind if I ask you questions, Danny?" I asked, carefully. He didn't know me from Adam, after all.

"That's your job, isn't it? Asking questions."

"It is. Let's start with Dix and Piglet. What can you tell me about them?"

He thought for a long moment and then began slowly. "It wasn't the first time they'd bought drugs from Duncan. They'd been around before. They weren't much older than I was. They didn't go to my high school, though." He shrugged. "I mean, I don't think they did. To be honest, I didn't go to my high school. Not really."

"You never heard last names or real names?"

"No."

"You never asked?"

"That wouldn't have been a good idea."

"What did they look like?"

"They were just guys, you know?"

"White guys?"

"I guess."

"You guess?"

"Um, it wasn't like it is in here. I mean, you didn't always know if someone was Latino or whether they were white, you know? In here, you have to know. You have to be careful that way."

I thought about that for a quick second. His life in this place was hard.

Very hard. But I couldn't think about that too much. It didn't matter. Not to the case.

"So, your brother said he didn't know anyone named Dix or Piglet. Why do you think he lied?"

"They wanted him to."

"The police?"

He nodded. "Yeah, the police."

"Any particular police?"

"There was one that came around. Duncan never told me his name. Said I was safer if I didn't know it."

"Do you remember what he—"

"No, I don't remember what he looked like. Honestly, I don't remember a lot. I was high most of the time."

"At the beginning of your interview with Commander Montero, you said your brother threw you out. Can you tell me why?"

"We had a fight. I remember that." Picking at the table in front of him with a fingernail, he said, "I think, I think it was about me stealing crack from him."

"You were pretty addicted by that point," I said.

He nodded.

"How many people was your brother selling drugs to? Roughly." I could feel Lydia look at me. My other questions had been pretty obvious. This one, not so much.

"I don't know. A lot."

"A hundred?"

"Yeah, probably."

"He had regulars? People who'd come every day?"

"Uh-huh."

"Do you remember any of their names?"

I slid the legal pad across the table with the pen on it, but Lydia stopped me part way. "No, they won't like that. Danny will tell you the names, you write them down."

Pulling the pad back, I looked across the room at the door that Danny had come through. There was a small window in it. I could see the guard watching us through it. That gave me the creeps.

"All right, Danny, who do you remember?"

"Um, Greg Pinney, Larry Tribble—he lived down the block, Kenny

Shoenecki—"

"Can you spell that?"

He shook his head. "I don't think so."

"Okay, you're doing good.

"Maria Costello and Melissa Costello, Terry Sweet—"

"Is that a boy or a girl."

"Boy. Brett Longoria. Noel something, Connors, I think."

He stopped. I waited. It didn't look like he was going to continue. I counted the names. Eight. Not terrible.

"Thanks Danny. Let's talk about Commander Montero." He looked a little confused. "The officer who took your confession."

"Oh yeah."

"I've watched the videotape. The interview actually began before the tape. Can you tell me what happened before the video was turned on?"

"I don't really know. It's sort of a blur."

"Montero says you spontaneously confessed."

"No. He's the one who kept talking about Audrey."

"Did he tell you what to say?"

"Not really."

"What does 'not really' mean?"

"He told me things, you know, like what happened to Audrey. Then he kind of acted like I told him."

"What about the drugs? Did he know you were smoking crack in the bathroom?"

"Dom, that's not important," Lydia said. "It won't help us."

"It helps me to know how far Montero was willing to go," I could tell she wanted to say more, but I turned back to Danny and asked, "He knew, didn't he?"

"I don't know. I just remember he kept saying if I told the truth everything would be okay. But he wouldn't let me tell the truth."

"Tell me about Audrey."

"Audrey was nice. I mean, we grew up together. She was always around, you know?"

"Was she doing drugs with the rest of you?"

He nodded.

"Did she have sex with a lot of the guys?"

"I don't think so. I don't think she liked guys much."

"Originally, you said she left with Dix and Piglet. Why do you think she left with them? What were they going to do?"

"Her grandmother bought her the new Nintendo. They were going to play Donkey Kong."

"So you think they went to Audrey's house?"

"I guess."

That didn't help. I doubted Audrey was killed in her own home. It would have helped to know where she was really killed.

"Can you think of anywhere else they might have gone?"

He shook his head.

"What about your attorney? Waterstone. Do you remember much about him?"

He picked at the table again. "I should remember him, shouldn't I? I don't really. I mean, I think I saw him three times."

"Three times? You only saw your attorney three times?"

"I think that's right. Is it perjury if I'm wrong?"

"This isn't a courtroom," Lydia said. "You're fine."

"Do you remember what you talked about with your attorney?"

"Isn't that a secret?"

"Not from us," Lydia said. "I'm your *new* attorney. Dom and I will keep your secrets."

"Do you remember what you talked about with Mr. Waterstone?" I prompted again.

"Kind of. Um, he asked about the people who came to the house. Just like you are."

"He asked about Dix and Piglet?"

"Uh-huh."

"And he thought they were real?"

"I think so."

When our time was nearly up, Lydia took over. She told him about the woman she was hiring as an expert witness to talk about false confessions. She spoke a little more about the legal process: which documents were being requested, which were being filed with the court. She also said, again, that it was her hope to shoot enough holes in the prosecution's case that they wouldn't even think about re-trying him.

He seemed to glaze over.

Lydia stopped. "Danny? We're doing the best we can to get you out of here."

He just shrugged.

"Don't you believe me?"

"I can't."

"You can't what?"

"Hope."

EIGHT

February 13, 1996
Late Tuesday afternoon

We drove out of our way to go to a Bob's Big Boy in Bakersfield. When Lydia said she knew a place she wanted to stop for a late lunch I thought she meant sushi or even Mexican. Middle-America greasy hamburger chain did not immediately come to mind.

Once we were settled in a red plastic booth studying the laminated menus, she asked, "What do you think you should do first?"

"I want to follow up on those names Danny gave us, maybe ask around at the trailer park—what's the name of that place?"

"Happy Acres."

"Okay, that's ironic. Um, I'll see if I can find any longtime residents. See who remembers what."

"And then?"

"Hopefully someone will remember Dix and Piglet. Hopefully there will be something to follow up."

Our waiter popped over. He was young, badly shaven and had a gigantic catsup stain on his white dress shirt.

"Hi, my name is Eric and I'll be your waiter," he said in a singsong. "Would you like to start out with a yummy root beer float?"

"Iced tea," Lydia said.

"I'll have a pop. Whichever kind of cola you have."

"I'll grab those for you and be right back!"

The minute he was gone, I asked Lydia, "Do you think he's a music major?"

"Why do you say that?"

"He practically sang to us."

"I didn't notice. I *did* notice that you said pop. Ronnie told me you're from the Midwest. He didn't say where though."

"Detroit. Have you been there?"

She shook her head. "I've heard it's rough."

"It is."

"Are your parents alive?"

"No. I'm afraid not."

Honestly, I wasn't sure if my parents were alive, but people looked at you pretty weird if you said something like that. Since this was not my favorite topic, I suggested, "We should look at Commander Montero."

She studied me, deciding whether to let me change the subject. Finally, she said, "Why do you think we should look at him?"

"Because he knows Danny was getting high. He knows the confession was a joke. Why was he okay with that?"

"Karen's been putting together everything that's out in public about him. Also, Vance Piper. I'll have her give you what she's got. We need to be very careful when we talk to people. I don't want anything to get back to them." She paused as though underlining the importance of that. "Then what? What else should you do?"

"Well, I'd like to find out who used Wite-Out on the DNA report."

"I've got Karen on them as well. Newspaper articles, public filings— did you know these *scientists* have websites now?"

I shook my head. I was a Luddite. I had an AOL account but barely used it.

Lydia continued, "We need to find the connection before we depose them. If someone asked them to alter the report, we need to know who before we get them on the record."

"Why? Why not just ask them?"

"Never ask questions you don't already know the answers to."

"You've said that before."

"It's still true," she said, raising an eyebrow to emphasize I should really remember the point.

Eric was back, setting our drinks down in front of us. "Do you know what you'd like for lunch?"

Lydia ordered an original combo with chili fries. I ordered a tuna melt with regular fries.

"Okie—I'll get those right out." Eric scooted away.

"I think it's pretty certain you'll get the conviction overturned, but what—"

"It's not certain. There are still judges who are reluctant to accept DNA evidence. They're dinosaurs, but they're out there."

I wasn't expecting that. I continued with my question, "So, what if you get the conviction overturned and the DA decides to prosecute Danny again?"

"Then we're at the mercy of the jury."

"But there's lots of reasonable doubt."

The O.J. trial had given the entire country a lesson in reasonable doubt. The defense claimed the LAPD were master conspirators and provided so-called evidence of that. They also claimed the LAPD were as inept as the Keystone Cops and provided—more convincing—evidence of that. In my mind though, the two theories could not coexist and cancelled each other out. The jury did not agree.

"There's also a lot of what I'd call reasonable suspicion," Lydia said.

"Explain, please."

"Normally reasonable suspicion is only applied to probable cause. A legal term for when you can search people without direct evidence. The thing is, juries and judges apply the principle all the time—they're not supposed to, but they do. For example, most people believe that if someone's been arrested for a crime, they're guilty. That's a reasonable suspicion that most of the jury will have coming in."

"Won't that be balanced out by the fact of the new trial?"

"Not if the ADA presents himself and his case in a logical and intelligent fashion."

"But you'll also present yourself in a logical and intelligent fashion."

"I'll be doing more than that. I'll be presenting myself as a John Grisham-style avenging angel."

"Shouldn't it really just come down to facts?"

"That would be nice, but what are facts, anyway? We'll put an expert on the stand to talk about DNA. They'll put an expert on the stand to throw doubt on our expert. We'll put an expert on the stand to talk about false confessions. They'll put an expert on the stand to refute what our expert says."

"Jesus," I said under my breath.

"That's why we have to go in with all guns loaded."

———

It was almost seven when I got home— we'd hit a lot of traffic passing downtown L.A. I apologized to Lydia, who had to drive back to Brentwood, but she shook it off. "I'm going to spend an hour or so at the office and then head back up when I'm sure there's no traffic. Dwayne's used to it. He needs time to read scripts anyway."

"Isn't that what he does at work?"

"God no. He takes meetings all day to talk about the scripts he reads on nights and weekends."

"So, it's not as glamorous as you'd think."

"It can be. He met with Mel Gibson last week. Mel wants to film the Bible." She rolled her eyes at that. I made a guttural groan and got out of her car.

When I walked into the house, I saw that Ronnie was sitting at the dining table with a stranger. A thin, angular man about my age wearing a white suit and a summer fedora. He looked like something out of *Casablanca*. Except that the man inside the suit had obvious wasting, deep indentations below his cheeks and a thickening of the skin. It was clear he was HIV-positive and that made him completely contemporary.

"Dom, this is Junior Clybourne. He's here about the room."

"Oh, nice to meet you," I said. "How did you hear about us." We'd been debating about placing an ad but hadn't yet.

"One of the waiters at The Bird." The Bird was another of the bars on The Stroll. I must have said something to a regular. That was how news spread, like a contagion. "I was just telling lovely Ronnie that I have a section eight voucher."

"Can we take those?" I asked.

Ronnie made a regretful face and shook his head. "No, unfortunately we can't."

"How do they work again?"

"I pay you a third of my income and then the government makes up the difference between that and the rent. I'm on disability because I have AIDS or *had* AIDS, I don't even know anymore. They started me on a new cocktail and I'm doing so, so well. AZT, ddC and saquinavir. *And* I'm starting a new trial at St. Mary's in a month. I think I might be able to go back to work next year. Of course, I can pay more rent in the event that I go back to work."

"What kind of work did you do?" I asked.

"Well, I worked at the harbor. In customs; not actually for Customs, I mean, I worked for a little firm that filled out paperwork for big foreign nationals. Mostly Chinese. I speak Chinese, you see."

"Mandarin or Cantonese?" Ronnie asked.

Junior said something I didn't understand. Ronnie said, "My mother would love you," so I assumed it was Cantonese.

"Junior's not your real name, is it?" I asked.

"It is. On my birth certificate and everything. Swear to God. I think my mother hated me even before I was born. Or my father. I could never work out which of us she hated more."

"Did Ronnie already show you the room?"

"He did. It's charming."

"It's small and doesn't get much of a cross breeze," Ronnie said, using his un-salesmanship. "I can make a few calls for you. I'm sure I know someone who'll rent you an entire apartment with your voucher."

"I don't have much, though. I really don't need all that space."

"Exactly how much is a third of your income?" I asked.

"I get eleven hundred and twenty-eight dollars a month disability, so, roughly, three hundred thirty-eight dollars and forty cents."

"Fine, we'll take that," I said, impulsively.

"Oh, aren't you an angel!"

"Dom, we agreed on five hundred. That's what John is paying."

"I won't breathe a word," Junior promised.

"It's okay. John won't mind. He's a nurse. I'm sure he'll be empathetic to your situation."

"He's a nurse! That's fabulous. You know, just in case. Listen, I'd like to move in as soon as possible. My current situation is less than ideal." In a stage whisper he said, "Straight people."

A moment later, he was saying "Ta-ta," and flying out the front door. The moment he was gone, Ronnie turned and gave me an evil eye that rivaled his mother's.

"What did you do?"

"He needs help."

"Didn't you hear me say I was going to make phone calls?"

"He doesn't want a whole apartment."

"I don't think I can get the section eight thing to work. I don't think they do roommate situations."

"It doesn't matter. Three eighty-eight is almost five hundred," I said.

"Your math is terrible."

"We'll be fine. We don't really need the money."

"Of course, we need the money. You know my plan," Ronnie said. "You know I want to have at least five rentals by the time I'm thirty-five. How am I going to do that if you give people discounts?"

"I just got a second job. I'll make up the difference."

"That's ridiculous."

"It's my money."

"Yes, and all you're doing is taking it out of one pocket and putting it into another."

"They're my pockets."

"They're our pockets, Dom. Ours."

For the first time, it occurred to me that I might have done something wrong. That maybe I really should have talked to Ronnie before lowering the guy's rent. That maybe I should have been more of a team player and not jumped in and made a decision.

"Look, sweetheart, I love that you're kind," he said. "I just get afraid you'll give away the store."

All right, so I knew where that was coming from. I'd been given a warning the year before about giving away too many free drinks at The Hawk.

"It's my fault. We should have talked about it first. We should have made the decision together.

"Oh," Ronnie seemed surprised. "Thank you."

He stood up and was about to leave the room, when he stopped himself and said, "And another thing. I wanted a flight attendant. Brad was wonderful. Wasn't he wonderful?"

Between his boyfriend and his job we barely got to know him, still I said, "He was wonderful."

"This guy doesn't even work. He'll be here all the time."

That was true. Ronnie was right, of course, so I tried changing the subject. "I'm starving. Is there any food?"

"There's leftover Thai food."

I got up and went into the kitchen. He followed me. I thought we were dropping it. We weren't.

"Flight attendants are gone two weeks out of the month," Ronnie reminded me. "What could be better than someone who pays rent every month and we never see them?"

"I'll get you a flight attendant for Christmas. I promise."

"My birthday's sooner."

NINE

February 14, 1996
Wednesday morning

Happy Acres sat in the crook between the intersection of the 405 and the 22. It was wedged in between an Oldsmobile dealership filled with large, gleaming new cars and a recent mini-mall that featured an ice-skating rink, a bakery, an ice cream shop, a check-cashing place and a bar called John Barleycorn's.

The trailer park was large. I drove all the way around it, which took nearly five minutes in minimal traffic. There were two entrances; I used the one right under the sign that read *Happy Acres Mobile Estates*. That created the amusing image of some two-story, five-bedroom manse being carted along behind an eighteen-wheeler.

When I pulled into the lot, I immediately saw I was right. There weren't any 'estates,' there were only single wides and doublewides in various states of disrepair. I randomly drove around until I came upon the office. It was stuck onto one end of what looked like might be a clubhouse. There was probably a pool behind it, I could definitely smell chlorine in the air.

After I parked the car, I walked over to the office and let myself in. A craggy old man looked up from behind a desk. Behind him were a couple of metal filing cabinets with a punchboard full of keys sitting on top of it.

"Help you?"

He had washed-out blue eyes that suggested he might have once been a looker.

"You the manager?"

He shook his head. "Owner. Artie Sarafin."

"How long have you owned this place?"

"*The Long Trailer*. Lucy and Desi."

"Excuse me?"

"Whenever that movie came out, that's the year I bought this place. I loved that movie. Sat in a theater up in Hollywood all day, watched it over and over. Then I went out and found this place. Eighty-five dollars an acre, can you believe that? Bought myself a trailer just like the one in the movie and started renting spaces. Everything was great until the sixties, when some politicians tried to get me out of here. So I sold off some acreage to the Oldsmobile people and greased the right palms. Happened again almost ten years later and that's how that skating rink place came about. Since then, they've left us alone. There's too many of us now."

A simple forty years would have sufficed, I didn't need his life story. I tried to get him back on track by asking, "Do you remember a girl named Audrey Gunderson?"

"That little girl who got herself dumped into a drainage ditch a ways back?"

"What do you remember about her?"

"Pretty little thing. Tomboy. That okay to say? People are getting kind of touchy about what you call them these days, but honestly I don't know what else to call the dyke-y ones."

"Tomboy's fine, I think. You remember a couple of boys who used the nicknames Dix and Piglet?"

"You have any idea how many teenagers been through this place since I started?"

"A lot, I'll bet. These would have been two kids hanging out with Duncan and Danny Osborne."

"Danny Osborne. He's the one killed that girl you asked about."

"He's the one who's in prison for it, but I don't think he did it," I said. "We did some DNA testing and it wasn't him."

A darkness seemed to come over him. "Naw, it was him. He confessed."

"He was a drug addict. He confessed to get his fix."

He shrugged. "Being a drug addict don't make you a liar."

"Look, I'm just trying to help an innocent kid. I'd like to talk to his neighbors. Any long-timers around who might have known Duncan and Danny?"

He turned around and pulled out an over-sized ledger from between the filing cabinets. He pushed everything on his desk aside to lay it down. He flipped through some pages.

Upside down, it looked like it was the place he kept track of who'd paid their rent and who hadn't. But it was also full of additional notes that I couldn't quite make out.

"Duncan Osborne was a drug dealer," I said, helpfully. "But I think you probably know that."

"I do," he said stiffly. "I wanted to run him out of here, but a policeman come by and told me to lay off."

"You remember the policeman's name?"

He shook his head. "I wrote it down though. I'll find it in a minute. The Osborne boys lived on Nevada Terrace."

He kept flipping through the book.

"How do I get to Nevada Terrace?"

"We're on Mississippi Parkway. You wanna go down that way," he said, pointing to his right. "Keep going past Nebraska Avenue down to Rhode Island Boulevard, turn left. Nevada Terrace is the first left from there."

I can't say that was clear at all, but it did tell me that the streets in the park were an illogical mishmash of state names. I figured I'd stumble around until I found it.

"Got it. Thanks." I lied.

"Here it is," he said, finding the name. Then he added, "Oh, this isn't going to help you much. Garcia."

"That's it?"

"Yup."

"No first name?"

It might not be that bad. Westmoreland didn't have a huge police department. And, it was Orange County. In the eighties it was pretty white. Of course, the officer might not have given his right name.

"Do you remember, when he came in, was Garcia in uniform? Did he show you his badge?"

"Maybe. I kind of remember that, but it might have been a TV show I saw about the same time."

I pulled the list of names out of my pocket and handed them over to him. "Could you look at these names and tell me if any of them still live here?"

He took the list and read through it. It only took a moment for him to say, "Some of these people never lived here."

"No? They probably live nearby, then?"

"Maybe. Couldn't say." He offered me the list. "There's a Tribble boy still lives here. The rest either don't anymore or never did."

"Where does Tribble live?"

"Rhode Island."

"You have a number?"

He shrugged. "I could look it up. But's it pink. You can't miss it."

"All right, well, thanks. If you don't mind, I might stop back in to see if you've remembered anything else."

"Oh, I think you should be happy I've remembered this much," he said. That sounded like he didn't want to talk to me anymore. I thought maybe I wouldn't stop back after all.

I left the office, got back in my Jeep, and drove off in the general direction he'd given me. It was easier if I ignored the ridiculous street names. I drove down two blocks and then took the next two lefts. That put me where I wanted to be on Nevada Terrace. I had the Osborne boys' address from the file and pulled up in front of it.

It was a bland-looking double-wide, unremarkable except that someone had had the bright idea to paint it a pale peach. In the driveway sat a sun-scorched minivan. Whoever lived there now probably didn't know a whole lot about the Osborne boys, so I looked up and down the street to see who else might be home.

Directly across the street sat a faded blue single wide from the early sixties. The driveway featured a faded, cherry red Honda Civic, and there was a garden on both sides of the stoop wilting in the harsh sunlight. I went over and knocked on the screen door. Bob Barker was making people guess how much things cost on a TV somewhere.

Then, a tall woman somewhere in her mid-fifties stood in the doorway looking me over. She had black hair—dyed, though not horribly—icy blue eyes, and a very shapely body. Her breasts were probably purchased, as they were much too pert for a woman of her age. She displayed them in a simple white tailored shirt, sleeveless. Honestly, I was tempted to warn her, "Be careful, you could put an eye out with those things."

"Well, look at you," she said. "If you're a traveling salesman, I'm definitely buying."

Great, this was going to be one of those conversations where I had to figure out a way to mention my boyfriend pretty quickly.

"I'm looking for people who knew the Osborne boys. Used to live across the street. Have you lived here long Mrs.—"

"Miss. You've caught me between husbands. But you can call me Peggy. And yes, I remember those boys."

"Can I talk to you about them?"

"Do I have to tell the truth?"

"It would help."

She swung the screen door open and I stepped in. Inside, the trailer was on the shabby side, desperately in need of rehab. "A freshening," as Ronnie would say.

"Can I get you an iced tea?"

"No, thank you. What can you tell me about the Osborne boys?"

Walking into the open kitchen, she poured herself a glass of tea then lit a cigarette, a skinny brown one. More was her brand. She shifted from one hip to the other. "What do you want to know?"

"You know that Danny's in prison for killing Audrey Gunderson?"

"Everyone knows that."

"I'm working for his lawyer. We've had a DNA test done and it showed that Danny didn't kill the girl."

"DNA. That's like genetics, right?"

"Sort of. It's like a fingerprint. When Danny was tried, they thought some pubic hairs found on Audrey's body were his, but they weren't."

"I didn't know Danny well. I mean, I lived here then, and I saw him around. I knew Duncan better, but that was after Danny went away."

Something in the way she said, "knew Duncan," tipped me off. "You and Duncan had a thing?"

Her eyes flashed. She hadn't expected me to pick that up. "Yeah, we did. And don't look at me like that. He was a bit younger than I am. Big deal."

I did some quick math. By a bit she meant two decades. I smiled at her, and said, "I have no room to talk, my boyfriend's still in his twenties."

She cocked and eyebrow and said, "Ah," as though I'd just explained something important.

"You knew Duncan was a drug dealer?" I asked.

With a shrug, she said, "It's like the second oldest profession."

"I haven't heard that one before."

"I made it up. Makes sense, though, don't you think?"

"I'd have said preacher was the second oldest. Did you have a drug problem?"

"I wouldn't call it a problem. And not while I was with Duncan. Those days were already behind me."

"Did Duncan ever talk about his brother?"

"Only if he had too much to drink."

"What did he say?"

"He felt bad about what his brother did. I mean, who wouldn't? Kind of blamed himself a little. He always thought the drugs were a big part of it. And he gave—well, mostly Danny stole them from him."

I wanted to stand on my head and scream bullshit, but I wasn't sure who was bullshitting me, Peggy or Duncan.

"You remember a couple of kids with the nicknames Dix and Piglet?"

"Oh, God, there were a lot of kids around and it was a long time ago. I mean, Piglet? That's some fat kid, right?"

"Maybe."

"There were a couple of fat boys hanging around. And Dix, that's a cock joke?"

I didn't laugh. "Could be a kid with the last name of Dix or Dixon or Dickinson."

"Oh, well... Do you want to borrow my phone book?"

I ignored that and asked, "There was a cop hanging around then, might have been protecting Duncan. His name was Garcia. Remember him?"

"Garcia? Seriously? I bet there are a hundred cops named Garcia in Southern California."

"I'm asking about one."

She shrugged in an unhelpful way.

I asked, "Who do you think killed Duncan?"

"Crips, Bloods, I don't know. Not the kind of thing you ask a lot of questions about. It's not safe, you know?"

"Were you still seeing Duncan when he was killed?"

"Not really."

"Does that mean yes?"

"That means we lived in the same trailer park. I *saw* him every once in a while."

I took out my trusty list of names. Offering it, I asked, "Do you remember any of these people?"

She squinted at it, too vain to wear reading glasses. A few seconds later she handed it back to me with a cold stare. If I didn't know better, I'd have thought she was trying to read my mind. "Nope, don't know any of them."

"Artie says Larry Tribble lives around the corner on Rhode Island. Pink trailer."

"Oh him. Yeah, I know him. They used to call him Trouble. He's like you."

"Like me?"

"Yeah, a gay."

I smiled and said "Thanks. I appreciate your candor." Of which I suspected there had been little.

"Why are the good ones always gay?" She sighed, almost under her breath.

I stopped and looked back at her, "Sorry to disappoint, but I'm not one of the good ones."

———

On Larry Tribble's kitchen wall hung a wrought iron and tile trivet that read: "Lord, grant me the serenity to accept the things I cannot change, courage to change the things I can, and the wisdom to know the difference." Which was a lot of words for a kitchen gadget.

He was a paper-thin guy who looked to be tightly wound. He'd let me in—probably because I had a red ribbon pinned to the collar of the vintage leather bomber jacket Ronnie had given to me for my last birthday. Larry led me to his eat-in kitchen. A kettle on the stove was boiling for tea. I smiled at him and asked my question again.

"Are you sure you don't remember Danny Osborne? Peggy over on Nevada Terrace said you would."

"Why does Peggy MacCallister think she knows who I remember and who I don't?"

"She said you're about the same age as Danny. And that you've lived here a long time."

"This used to be my parents' trailer. I moved back after they died." As advertised, it was a dusty pink single-wide with a pop-out. Inside, the appliances were turquoise, the walls a thin, yellow-y veneer and the floor gray linoleum. It was ancient but spotlessly clean. Perhaps that was how he honored his family.

"So, you must have gone to school with Danny?"

"I may have. I don't remember everyone I went to school with. Westmoreland High School has something like three thousand kids in its graduating class every year."

"But you would remember the boy who raped and murdered a girl just a few blocks from here, right?"

He frowned at me. "I didn't realize you meant *that* person."

The kettle began to whistle. He got up and made us cups of tea. I had the impression he regretted letting me in. Well, of course he regretted it. He was lying and it was obvious.

"Did you buy drugs from Duncan Osborne?"

"Do you take sugar?"

"No, thanks."

"Milk?"

I shook my head.

"Duncan. You used to buy drugs from him."

"I have my five-year chip. I don't think too much about the time before."

I sipped my tea and took another stab at getting information out of him. "When you were doing drugs and hanging out with the Osborne boys, do you remember a couple of guys named Dix and Piglet?"

"Isn't there something else we could talk about? Something nice?" He tried smiling at me. "There aren't a lot of gay people at Happy Acres and I don't get out as much as I—"

"Piglet was probably fat."

"No, he was—" Larry stopped, and his face flushed.

"So you remember Piglet?"

"Vaguely."

"Why was he called Piglet if he wasn't fat?"

"His father was a pig."

"A policeman?"

"Yes. A cop."

"What was his name?"

"I don't remember."

"Was it Garcia?"

"No."

"Then what was it?"

"I said I don't remember."

"I don't believe you," I said.

He shrugged. "Arrest me."

Of course, he knew perfectly well I couldn't arrest him. I might be seeking justice, but it was legal for him to obstruct it.

"What about Duncan? Peggy said he was killed by the gangs."

He nearly slipped again. A frown flashed across his face and he did his best to hide it.

"The gangs didn't kill Duncan?" I asked.

"I'm sure I have no idea. I know *I* had nothing to do with it. And that's all I know."

"I'm sure you've *heard* something. What have you heard?"

Abruptly, he stood. "I have a doctor's appointment. I forgot. I shouldn't have invited you in."

"I can come back," I said, sipping my teas as though I had no intention of leaving. "I'd really like you to tell me what you know."

"I told you, I don't know anything."

"A young man about your age is sitting in a prison cell expecting that he'll never get out. An innocent man. You can help him prove that. You can help get him out of prison."

"It's not my responsibility."

"Wouldn't you want someone to help you if you were in trouble?"

He drew himself up, stretching his head to the ceiling. "My dear, you can't possibly believe in white knights, can you?"

TEN

February 14, 1996
Wednesday afternoon

I knocked on a few more doors, several of which were slammed in my face, then gave up and started back to my Jeep. I was walking down Rhode Island Boulevard wondering if Peggy MacCallister had lied to me about Piglet's being fat or if she genuinely didn't know anyone named Piglet. I was pretty sure she was lying. She seemed too sharp to have forgotten.

Halfway down the street, I noticed an older gentleman sitting in a metal folding chair in front of an old Dodge Swinger. Next to him, on the concrete driveway, sat a cheesy, yellow boombox playing some improvisational jazz. I decided I'd approach this a bit differently than the first two people I talked to.

"That's the Köln concert, isn't it? Keith Jarrett."

"You like jazz?"

"I used to. I don't listen to it much anymore."

"That your Jeep down there?"

I nodded.

"Don't leave it there too long. They get nasty about parked cars."

"Thanks. How long you been sitting out here?"

"Maybe an hour."

"I didn't mean today."

"Oh. Few years. Sitting out here is better than watching soap operas."

"How long have you lived in the park?"

"Thirteen years, give or take? You with the census or something?"

I shook my head. "You remember the Osbornes?"

He stared at me. "Who are you?"

"Name's Dominick Reilly. I'm an investigator for Danny Osborne's attorney. We've tested some of the evidence and we believe Danny's innocent."

He nodded. "Yeah, I remember the Osbornes. Every one of them. The father, he got killed in a bar fight probably around the time we moved to the park. Then Danny raped and killed that girl in eighty-four—or at least he confessed to it. And Duncan, he was dealing drugs the whole time and then they killed him a couple years back. Crossed the wrong people I'd guess."

"Was there a mother?"

"Never saw her. We heard stories. Drug addict, speed I think, or whatever it was called back then. Can't say whether she's alive or dead."

"Do you remember any of Duncan's friends? Specifically, two named Dix and Piglet?"

A small, frail woman came out of the house and asked, "Wade, what's going on?"

"Nothing. Gentleman's just asking me some questions about the Osbornes. They're trying to get Danny out of prison. Where were we?"

"Dix and Piglet."

He glanced at his wife and said, "We never exactly socialized with the Osbornes, you know?"

She stepped forward and rested a hand on her husband's shoulder, saying, "We don't know anything about the Osbornes. Like my husband said, we weren't friendly."

"Peggy MacCallister told me she had a relationship with Duncan Osborne. Do you remember when that was?"

He said, "I think that started around the time the father died, so eighty-three, eighty-four."

"Wade. That's not our business."

But it was mine. Peggy had said she was involved with Duncan after Danny got sent to prison, which would have been sometime in eighty-six.

If what Wade said was true, it put her in the Duncan home around the time Audrey got killed.

"You remember a policeman named Garcia coming around?"

"I remember one named Sanchez," Wade said. "He came around once knocking on doors to make sure no one called the cops on the Osbornes."

The name didn't match but it sounded like the same person. I asked, "You hear any rumors about who killed Duncan?"

"Mexicans," Wade's wife said, without a thought.

"Why do you say that?" I asked.

"That's who he got his drugs from."

"Is it?"

"Well, I mean, I don't know that for sure."

"Who's dealing drugs in the park now?"

"No one."

"No one?"

Then Wade said, "There's usually a couple of kids out behind the skating rink. I'm pretty sure that's what they're doing."

His wife removed her hand as though she was repulsed by his knowing that. I was about to pull out my list of names for them to look at, but she said, "I'm sorry. We don't know anything. We can't help you."

———

"You got a card from your secret admirer," Ronnie said, when I walked in the door. He ignored that I held See's chocolates in one hand and a dozen roses in the other. "It's postmarked Springfield," he went on. "In Illinois. One of these days I'm going to open it up and see who it's from."

"Go ahead," I said.

The cards came for holidays. There was never a return address and they were never signed. Ronnie pouted as he read the card. They were usually funny, sometimes sappy, occasionally romantic. A couple of times a year, I sent unsigned cards back, though not as regularly as I received them.

"Show it to me."

Ronnie held up. On the front of the card was a yellow lab with a red rose in his mouth.

"What does it say inside?"

"'I woof you.'"

Winking at him, I said, "I woof you too."

He frowned at my joke. "Yes, but do you woof *him*?"

"I do. He's a *friend*. A dear friend."

I watched him think that over. I could tell he wanted to be angry, jealous about my having a mysterious far away friend. But it really wasn't tangible enough to be angry about.

"Don't you love your friends, Ronnie?"

"Sure. But I also talk about them. Use their names. Call them. Invite them over. *See* them."

I gave him a look and held out the gifts I'd brought. He grabbed the candy but left me holding the roses.

"Did you make a reservation at Massie's?"

"I did. But then I cancelled them when the card arrived."

"You didn't." We'd had the talk about the cards before, but it had never gotten serious. Never serious enough to cancel Valentine's Day.

"Actually, Junior is moving in tonight. I thought maybe we should be here."

He grabbed the roses then and went into the kitchen to put them in water. I followed. He stood at the sink filling a vase.

Sometimes I look at Ronnie and I'm completely and totally in love with him; other times the relationship is convenient—something I maintain for sex, mainly. And still other times it's about money. We've made a lot of money together—on paper, at least. And we'll make more. I'm a much richer man for having met Ronnie Chen. Actually, I'm a much richer man all the way around for having met him.

Ronnie set the flowers on the island between us.

"I went and talked to Danny's neighbors today."

"Did you?"

"Yeah. This one woman, she had some kind of relationship with Danny's brother. She lied to me. A lot. I don't know what that means."

"It depends on what she was lying about. Some lies are harmless."

I knew he told himself that about my lies. And they were *harmless*, perhaps more than harmless. I lied to protect him. To protect us. He seemed to know that. He seemed to believe it. At least, some of the time.

He got a bottle of fumé blanc out of the fridge. He poured two glasses and offered me one. When I hesitated, he said, "Come on, it's a holiday."

"Just one." I knew what he was up to. I was always drunk when I slipped up. I learned that early in our relationship and I'd stopped having more than one drink. Most of the time.

"So, what do the nicknames Dix and Piglet mean to you?" I asked him.

"Happy Valentine's Day to you, too."

"You wanted me to take the job. Now you have to suffer the consequences."

That made him smile. "Well, let's see. Piglet, baby pig, so it could mean someone fat but very young. Piglet is a character in *Winnie the Pooh* —oh, there's a guy at the gym with Tyger tattooed on his ass. Adorable!"

"His ass or the tattoo?"

"Both. It might be someone like that. With a thing for baby pigs. Or... it could mean the police. A brand-new cop, like a rookie."

"Or a policeman's child," I said. That was Larry Tribble's answer. Was it the right one?

"What about Dix?" Ronnie asked. "How are you spelling that?"

"I was thinking D-I-X."

"But it could be D-I-C-K-S?"

"It could be."

"Dicks and Piglet. Piglet and Dicks. Sex pigs? A sex pig and a diminutive sex pig? Could they be two gay guys buying drugs for a sex party?"

"It was the eighties, Danny's brother was selling crack."

"Hmmm... when did guys start using Tina?"

"Just a few years ago," I said.

"I think I was in college when I first heard about it. So, maybe late eighties."

"That's probably right. I don't think they're a couple of gay guys, though."

"No. Probably not. If they were gay, they wouldn't have raped and killed that girl. I mean, I suppose that's possible but very unlikely."

"True."

The doorbell rang. I followed Ronnie to the front door. When he opened it, we found Junior standing there wearing a moving man's coverall with a red Hermes scarf tied round his neck. Behind him, on 2nd Street, was a beat-up van and two rather rough looking young men.

"Thank God you're here! I forgot to ask for a key." He turned to the street and spoke to the young men in Spanish. They opened the back of the van and pulled out a large, red, uncomfortable looking Victorian sofa. We watched it being carried up the living room stairs.

"Isn't that awfully large for the bedroom?" Ronnie asked.

"You caught me," Junior said. "I'm a terrible size-queen. Wait until you see my bed. It's a four poster. E-nor-mous!"

And, a few minutes later, the bed passed by us. He was right. It was enormous. Ronnie and I shifted around, suddenly uncomfortable in our own home. *Should we help? Should we leave?* It was hard to decide exactly what to do.

"I should get his key," Ronnie said, and he went upstairs to the smallest of the bedrooms which he used as a home office.

Boxes on a metal hand truck went by. And then, much faster than I'd expected, Junior came down the stairs with the moving guys. He was chattering in Spanish and pulling envelopes of cash out of his overalls. At the door he said, "Gracias, darlings. Eres maravilloso."

The two guys nodded, clearly anxious to get to the truck and see how much was in the envelopes. I doubted Junior was able to tip. Although, if you'd asked me, I would have told you he'd have had to ask friends to help him move.

When he shut the front door, he turned and looked at me. "Come upstairs and chat while I unpack."

I wasn't entirely sure I wanted to do that, but I was curious to see how he'd fit his stuff into that bedroom. And I was right to be curious. In Junior's room, the sofa was pushed up against one wall. The bed needed to be put together, but it was easy to see—given the size of the headboard— that it was going to take up all by a foot or so of the remaining space. I didn't see how it would be a comfortable place to live since his choices were sitting on the uncomfortable sofa or reclining in bed.

He immediately began digging through the cardboard boxes stacked four-deep in all the corners.

"Eureka!" he exclaimed when he found what he wanted. He began unwrapping heavy crystal goblets. Handing me one, he said, "Look in that bag, dear. There's a bottle of Dom Perignon in there."

I raised an eyebrow. That was very expensive champagne.

"Don't give me that look. It was a gift. I have very generous friends."

Ronnie walked in. "Sorry, I had to return a couple of calls. Here are your keys to the house."

"Thank you! And here's your glass. We're having champagne as soon as your husband gets it out of that bag."

I went ahead and dug out the champagne. The bottle was still reasonably chilled. I popped it open. Luckily, it didn't spurt. I poured out three glasses. Mine was barely half a glass; I'd just have a taste. I mean, it was a holiday.

"I am so sorry to intrude on your Valentine's Day. I hope you didn't have to cancel plans."

"Don't worry, we were just on the verge of a tedious argument we've had before," Ronnie said.

Was that true? Had we been about to have an argument? It hadn't seemed that way.

"Well," Junior said. "Then I'm happy to have saved your evening." He raised his glass and said, "L'amore. L'amore. That's French for love."

I had the feeling he was quoting something, but I didn't know exactly what. We sipped our champagne. It was wonderful, though probably not worth what it cost. I could tell Ronnie was about to ask a polite question, but Junior interrupted him.

"I remember the first time I had champagne. I was barely sixteen when this film producer flew me to Las Vegas—breaking many federal laws and at least half the commandments. He introduced me to so many things. Champagne being my favorite. We stayed at the Sands. In their heyday. I hear they're tearing it down soon. Tragic. Simply tragic."

"Your parents let you fly off to Vegas?" Ronnie asked.

"Oh God no. I left home at fourteen, fifteen, somewhere in there. I lived by my wits, doing this and that." He smiled fondly at his memories. "I know it *sounds* horrid. But it really wasn't. Yes, I learned at a young age that there are terrible people in the world, but I also learned that most people are good. In fact, most people are *wonderful*. Like you two. I can tell already that you're both good people."

And who knows what to say to that. Luckily, John Gallagher stuck his head into the room. "Hello."

"Junior Clybourne this is John Gallagher," Ronnie made the introduction.

"Charmed, I'm sure," Junior said holding out his hand as though to be kissed.

John nodded, then said, "I've seen you around."

And that raised the question, *Why hadn't I seen him around? Did he not come into the Hawk? Or had I simply never noticed him?* Actually, he would be hard not to notice, so I had to assume he rarely came in.

"I hear we'll be sharing a bathroom," John said. "My towels are the blue ones." There were many other towels in the bathroom, mostly left over from previous roommates. "I usually shower before and after work."

"That's fine, darling. I'm more interested in afternoon baths with a good book."

"Perfect. Most of the time I'm asleep in the afternoon."

"Wonderful! We're going to be the best of friends."

I would have said they'd rarely see each other.

ELEVEN

February 15, 1996
Thursday morning

The next morning, I arrived at the Freedom Agenda before anyone else. That meant I had to hang around in front of the building until someone showed up. Karen pulled up at around nine twenty in a black Honda Prelude.

She didn't bother with good morning. Instead, as she unlocked the door, she said, "You're here early."

"Anxious to get started."

She gave me a look that suggested my enthusiasm was not appreciated, then she walked behind her desk. She shimmied out of her winter parka—she was the kind of Californian who considered anything under sixty to be arctic—and hung it on the back of her chair.

"Lydia said you were putting together information on Montero and the ADA?"

"Uh-huh."

"Can I look at what you found?"

"Sure. My computer just needs to boot up."

She'd already hit the power button for her PC and the printer. I was getting the impression she didn't like me much—or the fact of me, at least. I tried to smooth things over by asking, "So what do you think?"

"What do I think of what?"

"Of Montero and the ADA."

The computer finished booting up. She hit a few keys and a moment later the printer began spitting out paper.

"They're not crooked," Karen said. "I checked property records. Neither of them seems to be living above their means. Still, that doesn't mean they're good guys. I'd say they're both kind of political. Like, they'd do anything to get ahead. Well, Montero is retired. He was chief of police for Westmoreland the last two years of his career. The ADA on the case, Vance Piper, he's Chief ADA now. So he's moved up in the world. Probably wants to go higher."

"You think they're the sort who might bend the rules to get ahead?"

She gave me a look that suggested I was an idiot for even asking.

"Good to know." After a tiny pause I continued, "I have this list of names." From my pocket I took out the list of eight names Danny had given me. "I'm not exactly good at computers or I'd look them up, my—"

"It doesn't matter how good you are at computers. We don't have one for you. Besides, I use pay services to get my information. A firm downtown added us to their account. Everyone says you can surf the Net and find whatever you want, but it's really not like that if you're trying to do it for free."

I smiled and asked, "So, did you see *The Net* last year?"

"You're like the zillionth person to ask me about it."

"Oh, sorry."

"It was dumb. Really dumb."

"Ah, I see," I said, still holding out the list. Finally, she took it and glanced at it. Then she put it in her in-box. The printer stopped, and she took the pages out and set them on the desk. I reached for them, but she said, "Hold on."

She picked up a couple of manila folders, then organized the pages she'd just printed and slipped them into the files. Then she handed them to me. I thought for a moment about going all the way to the back and sitting on that horribly uncomfortable folding chair to read them, but I remembered how messed up my lower back had been Tuesday morning.

"Is Karpinski coming in today?"

"No. He's almost never here."

"Do you think it would be okay if I sat in his office?"

"He wouldn't like it."

I went out and sat across the street in my Jeep. I decided I'd look at the pages dedicated to Montero first. The top sheet was a 1993 article from *The Orange County Register*. The headline read: POLICE CHIEF CLAIMS CITY FORCING HIM TO RETIRE. The slug said, "Westmoreland Top Cop Alleges Unfair Firing."

Then the body:

Departing Westmoreland Chief of Police Samuel Montero has filed a claim against the city alleging he is being forced out of his position after objecting to city interference in police investigations.

The city denied the claims:

"The city wishes Chief Montero the best in his retirement," Westmoreland spokesperson Sharon Wiltmore said on Tuesday. "His service has always been valued."

Montero's claim, dated April 8, alleges that the city *"attempted to insert itself into investigations for political reasons and to sabotage the chief's authority."* In retaliation for Montero's objections, he was *"forced into a position where he had no choice but to retire."*

The claim did not go into detail about the allegations of interference, and Montero could not be reached for comment on Tuesday.

Montero's career with the Westmoreland Police Department began after he obtained an Associate of Arts degree in History from Long Beach Community College in 1971. He joined the Westmoreland Police Department and began what would turn into a remarkable career. In 1986, he received a Bachelor of Science in Criminal Justice from Cal State Long Beach.

During his twenty-two-year career with the department he was steadily promoted until becoming Chief of Police in 1991. He primarily worked as an investigator in the areas of homicide and narcotics. His involvement in several high-profile cases was thought to have contributed to his rise through the ranks.

City Hall sources, who've requested anonymity, suggest that issues surrounding Montero's investigations date back to the eighties.

I sat back and thought about what I'd just read. My first question was, *Did the lawsuit go anywhere?* Then I wondered about the final paragraph:

"...issues surrounding Montero's investigations." *What did that mean? Did Montero make a habit of coercing false confessions? Were there other innocent men in prison because of him?*

I turned to the next page. It was a crude list of names and addresses. Samuel Montero lived at 10705 Oakcliff Lane, 8809 Emerald Avenue, and 24681 Carnation Circle. All three addresses were in Westmoreland. It didn't say when he'd lived where but, below each address were other names. Someone named Debbie Williams lived at the Emerald Avenue address. She was either a wife, a sister or his mother. And someone named Sylvie Jacobson had lived with him at Carnation Circle. Sylvie Jacobson could also be a wife. Or a live-in girlfriend. I flipped ahead to see if Karen had gotten any marriage records. She had. Montero had been married three times. Susan Winslow in 1972, Debbie Williams in 1981 and Sylvie Jacobson in 1988.

The next items in the file were articles from *The Orange County Register* on a couple of the bigger cases Montero had worked. I skimmed through them looking for mentions of Montero. One of the cases was The Freeway Killer, active along the San Diego Freeway—though he did visit other freeways. Montero was mentioned in connection with a body dumped near the 405 in a location that wasn't far from where Audrey's body was found.

Another case, covered in a series of articles, was a woman who tried to say that a stranger had broken into her condo, killed her husband, and then raped her. A quick scan of the article suggested there were more holes in her story than Swiss cheese. Montero gathered evidence which led to a pretty tight case. Eventually he received a commendation for that work.

I sat quietly for a moment, making mental notes about what I'd read. Despite playing small roles in some high-profile cases, for most of Montero's career he was the kind of cop who'd bent the rules. I felt comfortable with this because of his behavior in Danny's case and the complaint he filed against the department. I was making a leap and I knew it, but I felt it was a pretty fair assessment.

Montero's personal life was something of a mess. Assuming he was still married to his third wife, since he'd managed to screw up two prior relationships. *Did he cheat? Did he lie?* I wondered what had happened. Of course, three marriages did not automatically make him a scoundrel. I'd had four major relationships and I was not a scoundrel—or at least not much of one.

I set Montero's file on the seat and opened Vance Piper's. The sheet on top of the pile was a printout from a website. Vance Piper had run for district attorney in November 1994. He'd lost but managed to keep his job as chief ADA. I continued to read:

A lifelong resident of Huntington Beach, Vance Piper grew up on the Southern California beaches, then earned a Bachelor of Arts in History at California State University, Fullerton, before going on to law school at UCLA. He has worked with the District Attorney's office in Orange County for nearly two decades.

In his cases, Piper has a reputation for fairness and following the letter of the law. He still resides in Huntington Beach and spends as much time as he can on a surfboard.

That last sentence struck me as odd. *Why did that matter?* Did his campaign people think people were more likely to vote for him if he surfed? He had to be well into his fifties. Was he really still surfing? Or did he just say so?

There were no wife or kids mentioned. They were big political assets, so they must not exist. And if they didn't, why didn't they?

Turning the page, I found myself looking at the same sort of address sheet that had been there for Montero. There was only one address and I was fairly certain it put him on the water. There were several other names associated with the address: Diane Piper, Helmut Piper and Craig Piper. Nothing told me whether these were a wife and children or a mother, father and sibling.

After that there were a few articles about cases Piper had prosecuted as an ADA. Before I could dive into them, there was a knock on the window of the Jeep. I glanced up and saw Lydia frowning at me. I rolled the window down. She was dressed a bit more casually, which probably meant she planned on staying in the office most of the day.

"What are you doing out here?"

"I wanted a comfortable place to sit."

"You could have sat in—" She stopped. Then she said, instead, "I'll have Karen find a comfortable chair for the back. Did you make it down to Westmoreland yesterday?"

"I did."

"And?"

"I got lied to a lot."

"Did you?"

"Yes. Woman named Peggy MacCallister had a thing with Duncan Osborne, but I think she lied to me about when. And then she lied about Piglet."

"Said she didn't know him?"

"Said he was a fat kid."

"That makes sense. Teenagers are cruel."

"Except this piglet was probably the child of a policeman."

"Oh, I see. Huh. I wonder if her lying means anything?"

"It could."

"Anything else?"

"There was a policeman floating around at the time. Uniform. Named Garcia or maybe Sanchez. Went around warning people off reporting Duncan."

"That fits with Duncan's being a CI."

"There's not a lot of agreement about who killed him. Though everyone connects it to his line of work."

"And why does that matter?"

"I don't know that it does. But it seemed worth asking questions. It could be connected to why he lied at his brother's trial."

She looked uncomfortable. "Try not to go too far afield."

I nodded.

"I have a dirty job for you."

I looked at her skeptically, "What's that?"

"I need you to go to Colin Waterstone's office and wait for him to give you Danny's files."

Given her attitude, I asked, "Does he know I'm coming?"

"No. That's why it's a dirty job."

She stood on her toes and looked me over through the Jeep's window. "You look too nice. Would you consider going home and putting on something a little...scarier?"

"How do you know I own anything 'scary'?"

She gave me the side-eye and said, "I'll call him a little after you get there."

I nodded and she gave me the address. Stopping at home, I changed into a BVD T-shirt and a black motorcycle jacket I hadn't worn in years. There were snapping leather epaulettes on each shoulder into one of which I'd put a metal cock ring. It pinched, so it was more useful as decoration. I hoped this look was challenging enough to get what we wanted.

Then I got on the 5 and drove down to Irvine. Waterstone's office was in a black glass building near John Wayne Airport. There was a giant parking lot across the street, and between that and the building stood a battalion of palm trees. I parked, found the lobby and got directions from a security guard.

On my way up to the sixth floor, I thought about how to approach this. If I presented myself as Lydia's investigator and asked for the files, they'd tell me they weren't ready. I'd tell them I'd wait. They'd tell me not to. I'd tell I didn't mind. That would escalate until they called security. That wasn't going to work. So, what *would* work?

I walked into the reception area of Cotter, Washington, Lane and Butler. A pretty young boy of about twenty-one sat at a large desk with a giant multiline phone. He looked clueless enough to be related to someone important at the firm. That would work in my favor.

The waiting room was full of men in expensive suits. That, too, would help me.

"I'm here to see Colin," I told pretty boy.

"Colin Waterstone?"

"I guess that's his last name. Do you have a lot of Colin's to choose from?"

"Who should I tell him is here?"

I leaned forward and said, "Describe me. He'll know."

Pretty Boy picked up the phone and dialed an extension. While he spoke to whomever on the other end, I turned and took in the waiting room. No one would look at me; I was making an impression. Which was exactly what I wanted.

I heard Pretty Boy set the phone down and turned back to him.

"He'll be right out."

"Thank you," I said, winking at him. He didn't know what to do with that.

There were no empty seats, so I stood there in front of the receptionist's desk. The reception area was nicely paneled with leather furniture and a deep carpet. This was a nice firm. For the first time, I wondered what

Colin Waterstone was doing there. He'd been a public defender when he represented Danny. He'd come up in the world.

A decent-looking guy in his early forties came into the waiting room. He had sandy brown hair, a thin, angular face and was nearly as tall as I am.

"Can I help you?"

"It's good to see you, Colin."

"I'm sorry, I don't think we've met."

"Don't be like that. We met at Danny Osborne's party last weekend. You remember. You weren't *that* drunk!"

He stared at me a moment, decoding what I'd said. Under his breath he said, "Lydia Gonsalez. All right, follow me."

I followed him to an office in the middle of the floor with a view of the building next door. Obviously, he was still working his way up. Outside his office, in the center part of the floor, was a field of cubicles set up in such a way that I wasn't sure whether he had his own secretary or not. When we were inside his office, Colin shut the door.

"Tell Lydia she's a bitch."

I decided I wouldn't do that, but there was no reason for him to know. "Do you have Danny's file?"

He picked up Danny's file and held it out to me. "She's claiming ineffective assistance of counsel, isn't she?"

"He's innocent." Given that, it seemed obvious his counsel was ineffective.

"He's innocent based on information that wasn't available at the time. I did the best with what I had to work with."

I sensed an opportunity here, so as I took the file from him, I asked, "Would you tell me about the case? I'd like to hear your side of things."

"I did the best I could for that kid. I got him an amazing deal and he wouldn't take it. Voluntary manslaughter. He'd have been out a couple years ago."

"Wait a minute. A girl was raped and murdered, and the DA offered voluntary manslaughter? That's ridiculous." You didn't need a law degree to know that was an absurd deal. Rape. Murder.

"I know. All Danny had to do was say he'd been taking dope and lost control."

"They must not have thought much of their case."

"They actually had a good case. Juries usually believe confessions, no matter how far-fetched."

"Not to mention his brother testifying against him."

"Well, yes, that was unexpected."

"Do you know anything about Duncan being a confidential informant for the Westmoreland police?"

"No, I don't. I think it highly unlikely, though."

"Why is that?"

"It just is."

"The prosecution would have disclosed it?"

"No. They wouldn't have to. He wasn't testifying as a CI. He was testifying as a brother."

"They still could have put pressure on him."

He bristled. "You're suggesting some kind of conspiracy. Why would the police and the DA conspire to put an innocent kid behind bars?"

"Actually, that sounds like a question you should have been asking when you defended him."

And then he threw me out.

TWELVE

February 15, 1996
Thursday afternoon

Back at the Freedom Agenda, I was heading toward Lydia's office when Karen stopped me with: "You know a lot of dead people."

"Do I?"

"That list you gave me, five of them are dead."

That did make sense. There's a high mortality rate among drug addicts. "Did you get cause of death on any of them?"

"Three overdoses. One AIDS. And one murder."

"What about the three living? What did you find on them?"

"I have addresses for Noel Connor and Maria Costello. There's no death certificate for Melissa Costello, but she also doesn't seem to live anywhere. I'm thinking homeless?"

"Thanks," I said. I was about to go into Lydia's office when I realized something important. "What about Larry Tribble? He's not dead."

"Yes, he is."

"I saw him yesterday. I asked him questions."

She flipped through some papers in front of her. "He died five years ago. In July of 1991."

"He's living in a pink trailer at Happy Acres. On Rhode Island Avenue."

She looked at her paper again. "Yes. That's where he *was*."

"Okay," I said. "I guess I'll have to figure that one out."

"Maybe you interviewed a ghost," she said dryly.

"Yeah, I kind of doubt that. Thanks."

Then I brought Danny's file into Lydia's office. She practically snatched it out of my hand. I started to leave her alone with it, but she said, "No, no, sit down."

I took a seat as she scanned the file.

"Did you have trouble getting it?"

"No, he handed it right over."

"Oh good. I'll have to send him a thank-you note."

"I don't know if I'd bother. He said to call you a bitch." I hadn't planned to tell her that, but he was kind of a dick.

Looking up, she said, "Well, now I know how to sign the note." She went back to reading the file.

"I talked to him a little about the case. Danny was offered voluntary manslaughter. Waterstone was very proud of that."

"That's—they couldn't have offered that. Not for the rape and murder of a teenaged girl," she said, stating what I'd already assumed. She flipped quickly through the file. "Okay, here. There's a note that a plea bargain was offered but turned down by the client. It doesn't say what the offer was though."

"Will it be in discovery?"

"Probably not. It would have been verbal. I doubt they would have committed an offer that bad to paper. Still, if I were Waterstone, I would have come right back to my office and outlined the deal in a memo just to get it on paper."

She continued to look through the file. The speed at which she was able to glance at a document and get some sense of what it meant was impressive. "There's nothing in here."

"Do you think he lied to me?" I asked. It didn't seem outside the realm of possibility.

"He's very concerned about his image."

"Well, he's moved up in the world," I said. "That's a nice firm he's working for."

"Is it? Hmm." She set the file down. "There's not much in the file, at all. That alone should justify ineffectiveness of counsel."

"But it won't?" I guessed.

"No. Judges are loath to do that to public defenders. A public defender can fall asleep and a judge might not grant a new trial based on ineffective counsel."

That seemed kind of crazy, so I asked, "Is there a reason for that?"

"The last thing a judge wants to do is assign counsel. Attacking the public defenders is not a good idea since that could put them in a position where they have to grab counsel from the hallways. Nobody wants that."

"You're saying ineffective counsel isn't going to get Danny a new trial no matter what. Why is Waterstone so freaked out, then?"

"Just because it won't get Danny a new trial doesn't mean we won't go on and on about it. We're throwing everything against the wall and seeing what sticks."

"So, Waterstone is upset because you're going to trot out his bad behavior in front of a judge?"

"And... it'll be public record."

"The files I read this morning; I have two questions." And they were both questions Waterstone should have asked.

"Shoot."

"Why? Why did Montero do such a crap job with this? From his file he seems to have done a good job on some high-profile cases, so he's not inept. He had to have known Danny was innocent, but he makes his case anyway."

She didn't say anything, so I continued. "In my experience, cops are only bad for a few reasons: Greed. Ambition. Peer pressure. *And* covering up their own corruption. But none of those seem in play here."

As soon as I finished, I realized what I'd done. I'd made it clear that I knew cops and knew them well. Lydia was still flipping through Danny's file, what there was of it. She didn't react. Didn't look up or suddenly yell *A-ha!* After a moment, she asked, "You said you had two questions. What's the second one?"

"Why did Vance Piper go along with it?"

"You think they're connected? That whatever way Montero is bad, Piper is too?"

"I'm starting to think that, yeah."

"Don't get caught up in that. We'll never have to show *why* they're corrupt or even that they're corrupt together—they're not on trial. We just need to show that they *are* corrupt."

I stewed on that. There were many things about the law I didn't like. It's willingness to not know things was one of them. I took a deep breath and asked, "What's next?"

"The transcript arrived. We'll start reading in the morning. Bring your reading glasses."

———

Even though Ronnie saw clients in the evenings and on weekends, he always tried to keep Thursdays open for us and pushed as many clients as he could into my three-day work week. It was no surprise to find him at home when I got back from the Freedom Agenda. What was surprising was to find him on our tiny front lawn arguing with his mother. Next to Mai, stood a thick-waisted Asian girl in a pink skirt and green top. She looked miserable. Also on my front lawn was Junior Clybourne.

I parked the Jeep and walked back down to my house. Junior picked that moment to begin speaking to Mai in Cantonese. At first she looked confused, but then her eyes flared with anger. She unleashed a torrent of Cantonese which—even without a translation—can best be described as ripping Junior a new one. Then she grabbed the girl like she was a bag of luggage and climbed into her black Jaguar XJ.

"I'm so sorry," Junior was saying to Ronnie. "I thought I was helping. I don't know what I said that made her so angry."

"What just happened?" I asked.

"That girl went to the movies with us a couple of months ago and now she's agreed to marry me. And Junior tried to help—"

"I said something wrong; I can't imagine what it was."

"You implied that my mother had needed to marry my father as though she was a village girl or a bar girl."

"Oh dear, I assumed, didn't I?"

"My mother's family owned many businesses and a lot of property in Saigon. My father met her while he was attached to the diplomatic service."

"Ah... I thought she was like that poor girl. I thought she was trying to help her because they were the same," Junior said. "I should not have stuck my nose in. I'm so, so sorry."

"It's fine," Ronnie said. I could tell that it wasn't.

"You know, this is just like *The Wedding Banquet*! I loved that film. Did you love that film?"

Ronnie gave him a dark look; darker than any I'd seen in a long time. "No, I did *not*."

"Oh. Well. You'll have to tell me everything you hated about it."

"We should go have dinner," I said to Ronnie.

"Oh, that's sounds lovely," Junior said, misunderstanding me.

"I think just Ronnie and me."

"Of course, no need for a third wheel." Finally taking his cue, he said, "Well, you two have a lovely evening."

He went back into the house. I watched Ronnie's face. "Do you need to grab anything?"

"No, I'm fine."

"Then let's go."

Twenty minutes later we were sitting in The Bird, which was half bar and half restaurant. There was a mirrored wall behind the bar and an exposed brick one in the dining room. The other walls were sage green with lavender highlights. One boasted a giant purple painting of Greta Garbo. The menu focused on gourmet comfort food: meatloaf, and macaroni and cheese.

Ronnie's cosmo arrived and he took a sip. Then he said, "She has to stop. I'm going to tell her that if she doesn't stop, I won't see her anymore."

"I don't think you really want to do that."

"Be on my side, Dom, please."

"I am on your side. It's going to hurt you if you stop seeing your mother."

"I can't take it. All these poor girls she talks into meeting me. I don't even know where she finds them, but they come expecting... well, not me."

I didn't say anything, just sipped my soda water.

"I think this one's a lesbian. I think that's why she's willing to marry me." He drank his drink. "Why can't my mother just love me for who I am? It's like she only loves the person she wants me to be."

"I don't think that's fair. She wants what she *thinks* is best for you. The fact that she's wrong doesn't mean she loves you any less."

He considered and drank his drink. "How do I get her to understand she's wrong? I don't think she's been wrong about anything in her life."

"Time. You just have to give it time."

THIRTEEN

February 16, 1996
Friday morning

It promised to be a long day. I arrived at The Freedom Agenda around nine. I'd be able to stay until four, then I had to go home and change for my shift at the Hawk. I started at six and would work until at least three in the morning. Last call was at one thirty. The alcohol had to be off the bar by two. Then I had to throw everyone out and clean up. I would be pretty exhausted by the time I got home.

When I walked into the office, I saw Karen's sweater on the back of her chair and heard the copy machine chugging away in the back room. I went back and found her stacking three ream-sized piles of paper. Danny's transcripts. And the copier was still going.

She looked up and gave me a surly glare. I knew I should have stopped at Albertson's for an Entenmann's coffee cake. I hadn't because that would have added a half an hour to an already long day. Now I felt like it would have been worth it.

I went over and poured myself a coffee—thankfully the pot was still half full, so I didn't have to fuss with making a new one. The coffee was every bit as dreadful as it was on my first day there, but it was still free.

"Can I start?" I asked. Karen looked annoyed—I was messing with her neat but unfinished piles—still, she handed me one of the stacks. I went over to the other table and sat down in the ungodly metal folding chair. Karen hadn't found me a more comfortable chair. I was going to regret this in a few hours.

"I got some information on that Larry Tribble guy," Karen said.

"Yeah?"

"Leonard Tribble worked for Cal Research right up until 1991. It's a company that does telephone polls. I called them. They said Leonard Tribble was legally blind."

"They say what happened to him?"

"He just stopped showing up for work. About five years ago."

"If he's legally blind would he be getting a disability check in addition to his paycheck?"

"I'd have to double-check, but he might be."

"So, just guessing here... Leonard Tribble dies, and his brother gets his own name put on the death certificate and collects his brother's disability." I thought for a moment—*how did this help Danny?*—and then I remembered Larry Tribble had been less than truthful. I now had a weapon to force the truth out of him.

"Thanks Karen, that's a big help."

That very nearly earned me a smile. I began flipping through the stack of paper in front of me. A lot of it was basically incomprehensible, or worse, useless. Quickly, I saw that the transcript included all the pretrial motions. They weren't really interesting. After each appearance there was an index. I stopped.

What was the most important thing I wanted to know? Duncan. I wanted to read Duncan's testimony. I began flipping through the pages looking for his name. I found it about halfway through the ream. I skimmed through looking for questions I wanted answered. Piper asked him, *"Why did you throw your brother out?"*

"He is... was, he was a drug addict. I thought it might be the only way I could help him."

That was true and not true at the same time. Yes, of course, Danny was a drug addict, but he got his drugs from his brother. Duncan's answer implies that he had no part in Danny's addiction.

I kept skimming until I found this from Piper examination:

Q: Did you see your brother leave with Audrey Gunderson?

A: I did.

Q: What time was that?

A: In the afternoon. I guess around four. Maybe a little a later.

Q: Was anyone else there?

A: No.

Q: There were no boys named Dix and Piglet?

A: No.

That was smart of Piper to get Duncan's denial out there first. I flipped a few pages to see what Waterstone had to say about it. He asked,

Q: What do you do for a living, Duncan?

A: I pick up odd jobs here and there.

Q: Is dealing drugs an odd job?

Piper made an objection.

THE COURT: Mr. Waterstone, even if the witness is a drug dealer, he's not going to admit it in open court. Move on, please.

Q: A lot of people come to your home, isn't that right?

A: Yeah, I'm kind of popular.

Q: So, there could have been a lot of people at your home the day Audrey was killed.

A: I suppose. I don't keep track.

Q: If you don't keep track of who's in your home, how do you know no one named Dix or Piglet was there?

A: Well, I don't really know everyone who comes by.

Q: Because you're so popular.

A: Yeah, I guess.

Q: Where did you brother get drugs?

A: Around.

Q: So, you weren't the only drug dealer in Happy Acres?

Piper made another objection. They went round and round. The judge seemed unhappy with all the drug talk reminding everyone, *"This is a murder trial. Not a drug trial."*

THE COURT: Do you have any more questions, Mr. Waterstone?

ATTORNEY WATERSTONE: No, your honor.

I thought it odd that it was over so soon. Waterstone had barely asked anything. He could have asked, was Duncan working with the police? Or, why he was lying? Well, no, he probably couldn't have asked those things. But they were questions I'd like answers to.

I circled back looking for Montero's testimony. When I found it, it began with Piper laying the groundwork for the tape. He asked if it was common to record interviews. Montero said it was. Piper offered the edited tape into evidence.

I stopped; then flipped back to the pretrial motions. There was one that pertained to the editing of the videotape. Apparently, the video went on for nearly fourteen hours. The judge agreed to having it edited as long as the complete footage was provided to the defense. In the event that exculpatory evidence was found on the footage, the defense would be allowed to present it. Somehow, I doubted Waterstone had watched the entire fourteen hours of video. My guess was he hadn't spent a total of fourteen hours on the whole case.

Then, I found Waterstone's cross-examination of Montero.

Q: Commander Montero, you stated that you brought the defendant in for questioning on April nineteenth of last year.

A: That is correct.

Q: Why?

A: I'm sorry, I don't understand the question.

Q: Why did you bring Daniel Osborne in for questioning.

A: Oh. We were reconstructing the Gunderson girl's day and learned that she was at the Osborne residence that afternoon.

Q: So, you questioned Duncan Osborne and then Daniel. Is that right?

A: No. We questioned Danny first.

Q: Why? Why not Duncan? He's the owner of the home.

A: Danny is about the Gunderson girl's age. It seemed a good idea to start with him.

Q: Because girls are more likely to experience violence from boys their own age?

A: I don't—that's not what I said. We thought Danny might have a closer relationship with the girl.

Q: Because teenage girls prefer boys of their own age?

A: I really don't know what teenage girls prefer. I have a son.

Q: Were there any other lines of investigation you pursued?

A: Danny came to our attention early on.

Q: So, you didn't look for any boys with the nicknames Dix and Piglet?

A: Danny is the only one who—

The bell rang at the front of the storefront as someone came in. A moment later Lydia was in the back with us mid-sentence.

"—awful. The 405 is a parking lot all the way to the 710. I did manage to get a line on a painter though. I can't wait until we move into the house."

"Isn't your husband going to hate the drive?" Karen asked.

"I think traffic is better in that direction."

I was fairly certain it was just the opposite.

"Is that the transcript?" Lydia asked, then without waiting for an answer picked it up. "Have you found anything interesting?"

"Everyone seemed to know Duncan was a drug dealer and no one seemed to care."

She thought that over for a moment. "Any suggestion he might have been the one to actually kill Audrey?"

"Not that I've found. Do you really think he might have been the one who killed her?"

"No. But it could make a credible alternative. Certainly, it would explain the hair analysis."

"Wasn't that kind of evidence discredited?" I asked. I did read the newspaper, after all.

"Not completely. At the time, it was used to exclude a suspect. So if it's similar to Danny's then it could be Duncan's."

"The hair expert is about halfway through," Karen said.

"Okay. I'll be in my office."

Lydia walked away. Karen turned off the copy machine, picked up the rest of my copy, and handed it to me. Then, taking her own stack, went out to her desk at the front.

I opened my ream to the halfway point and began looking for the forensic hair analysis. I found it. The first few pages were Piper fawning all over the guy—whose name was Denton Fisher—proving that he knew everything he was talking about. He did have a respectable number of college degrees.

Thinking I might get more out of the cross examination, I flipped forward until I found Waterstone's name.

Q: Mister Fisher.

A: Dr. Fisher.

Q: My mistake. Dr. Fisher, you testified earlier that the pubic hair found on Audrey Gunderson's body is close enough to the defendant's that you feel confident of a match. Could you put a numeric value on that?

A: I really don't think that's—

Q; Indulge me.

A: Well, eighty percent.

Q: So, you're eighty percent certain that the hair found on the victim is the defendant's.

A: Yes.

Q: That means then that you're twenty percent uncertain.

A: I don't think about it that way.

Q: For every eighty times you're right, you're wrong twenty. Correct?

A: That's not how I look at it.

Q: What if Danny Osborne is one in twenty? What if you're wrong about him and that's not his hair found on the victim.

A: In the victim's mouth. The hair was found in the victim's mouth.

Q: Yes. I understand that.

I had to stop reading. I couldn't think about that poor girl and how she was found. It was too much. The connections—not to mention my hip was killing me and my upper back. I wasn't going to be able to sit on that chair all day.

Putting my copy of the transcript onto the long table where I'd sorted letters from possibly innocent men, I walked out to the front. Lydia was on the phone when I passed, so I told Karen, "I have to run an errand. I'll be back in forty-five minutes." I didn't give her the chance to say anything about it.

In my Jeep, I drove across the city to the Staples near the traffic circle. I spent nearly three hundred dollars on a chair that at least looked like I'd be able to sit in all day long. The box was pretty big, so one of the clerks helped me with it to the Jeep and we jockeyed it into the back seat—well, partly in the back seat and partly in the passenger seat.

On the way back, I thought about stopping at home. Ronnie had still been asleep when I got up. He'd been up quite late, drinking a bottle of wine, on the phone bitching with friends about his horrible mother. I wished there was a way for me to fix things between them—but this was theirs. There wasn't much I could do. I decided against stopping in and when back to work.

Carrying the box into the office got me a look from Karen. I answered it with, "Chair." In the back, I opened the box and looked around for the instructions. Like so many things these days, it didn't use words, it used pictures. Fortunately, it was really only a matter of putting together three partly assembled pieces. I was nearly finished when Lydia came up to me.

"I'm sorry. I forgot to tell Karen to get you a chair. Don't be annoyed with her."

I wondered if that was true or not.

"Do you have the receipt?"

"Don't worry about it."

"No, I should pay for it. We should have taken care of this right away."

I sat down in the chair. It was much better. I realized I must be getting old if a chair meant this much to me. Of course, I wasn't going to let Lydia pay for it, so I asked, "Since you're here, can I ask a couple question about Danny's case?"

She smiled. "You're very involved, aren't you?"

"What?"

"To most of us it's the Osborne case. To you it's Danny's case."

"Is that bad?"

"No. It's why I hired you."

But she had no reason to think I'd get this involved; she'd only just met me. I could have pushed her on that, asked why she was so sure of who I was, but I wasn't sure I was ready for the answer. Instead I asked, "Why didn't Waterstone have his own hair expert?"

"They cost a lot of money. He would have had to motion to have the court pay for it. It would have been a hassle, so he didn't bother."

"Do you remember when they offered the deal? Was it before the trial or during?"

"During."

"Do you have any idea when?"

"Waterstone's note was dated February fourth."

I was impressed that she remembered without having to go back to the file. I picked up the transcript from the folding table next to me, cut the stack in about half, and began looking at the dates.

Lydia saw what I was doing, and said, "The prosecution rested that afternoon. The judge called a recess until the following week."

Okay, now that was creepy. "You just got the transcript an hour ago."

"I start by creating a timeline. I want to get a feeling for the trial as a whole. The motions. How many days did the prosecution take? How long was the defense? That sort of thing."

"Oh, I've just been jumping around, reading testimony." I felt kind of dumb.

"That's great. I don't want you thinking like me, that would be pointless."

She had a point.

"Why do you think they offered the deal at that point? Was their case that weak?"

"I'll have to go over it more closely, but I wouldn't say it was weak—aside from the fact they were prosecuting an innocent man."

"Then there must have been something in the defense's case they didn't want coming out."

"Yes. That's entirely possible."

FOURTEEN

I felt good. Happy even. Digging into Danny's case, figuring things out, made me feel like I was doing something that mattered. I was helping someone innocent. And possibly, maybe, finding the person who'd killed poor Audrey. It made me feel alive in a way I'd almost forgotten.

I spent the rest of my time at the Freedom Agenda that day reading the defense's case. I finished about twenty minutes before it was time for me to leave. Not because I'm some super speed reader, but because there wasn't a whole lot there. Only five witnesses: Sue Gunderson—Audrey's sister, Wade Lovett—the man I talked to who lived across the street, Cameron Ford, William Peterson and Wendy Dalworthy.

Sue Gunderson testified to the fact that the police never impounded her car. They never searched it for evidence. Ever. In Danny's supposed confession, he borrowed her car to take Audrey's body to the culvert. But there's no proof of that when there could have been if they'd searched the car. So why didn't they?

In his cross, Piper acknowledged that it was poor police work and asked Sue if she thought that meant Danny didn't kill her sister. Her answer was rather succinct: "No. He killed her."

Lovett testified that he'd seen Audrey leaving the Osborne home with two teenage boys, neither of whom were Danny Osborne. On cross, Piper attempted to confuse him, to get him to mix up the time frame, to suggest he didn't see what he saw. But Lovett held to what he saw. He was probably the best witness for the defense.

When I'd met Lovett the other day, he'd been less than forthcoming. I wondered why. Was something at risk? Was there something for Lovett and his wife to be afraid of? He could have easily told me what he'd seen but he hadn't. He'd carefully avoided it. I went back to the transcript.

Sixteen-year-old Wendy Dalworthy took the stand. Mostly, she was a character witness, testifying that Danny was a sweet boy and that he would never hurt anyone—in her opinion. Piper had her in tears admitting that she really didn't know Danny that well and had barely seen him since he began taking drugs.

Cameron Ford was one of Duncan's clients. When Waterstone attempted to bring that out, the DA objected and the judge agreed. Then the judge asked if Cameron had been there the day Audrey was killed. He had not. The judge dismissed him before Waterstone had an opportunity to ask about Dix and Piglet.

Finally, and definitely least of all, was an elderly gentleman named William Peterson who claimed he saw two teenage boys in a car matching the description of Sue Gunderson's car. Piper attacked Peterson's credibility by talking about the prescription in his eyeglasses, which Peterson said was just fine. At the end of the testimony Piper held up a photo and asked, "Is this one of the boys you saw?"

"It might be."

"It's a picture of Tony Danza, an actor on *Who's the Boss*?"

And that was the end of his credibility.

After the Freedom Agenda, I stopped at home to change into my regular bartending uniform: 501s and a black T-shirt. Ronnie came into the bedroom after I showered. His face glum.

"I finally did it."

"Did what?" I asked. Hoping he meant he'd finally sold some house that had been hanging around forever but knowing that's probably not what he meant.

"I dumped her. Told her I didn't want to see her anymore."

"Your mother?"

"Of course, my mother."

I dried myself for a moment. "Okay."

"You think I'm wrong, don't you?"

"No. I think you might regret it someday."

"It won't go on that long. She'll cave."

I didn't know what he was basing that on. "And if she doesn't?"

"I can't go on like this. She doesn't want to be part of my life."

"Yes, she does."

"No. She wants to be part of the life she wants me to have. That's different."

I had to admit there was some truth to that. Mai was ruining her relationship with the son she had for the son she wished she had. It was a terrible situation. I went over and hugged him.

"Maybe you're right. Maybe she'll come around."

It was Friday, so The Hawk was busy. I didn't have much time to think about Ronnie's trouble with his mom or Danny's case. There was a second bartender for the most of my shift. A guy named Robbie, who was a body builder and wore nothing but a pair of partly unbuttoned overalls. He flirted with the customers at the bar while I took care of the service line. Fortunately, we were splitting tips.

Robbie's shift was over at midnight. Generally, he took one of his customers home with him. His taste ran to chunky, middle-aged bears, which often disappointed some pretty young thing waiting around, convinced he was Cinderella for the night. I usually soothed the outrage with a free shot.

I called last call and began collecting drinks. By then, I'd done most of my side work. It took fifteen to twenty minutes to do the drawer, which was about as long as *sidewalk sale*. Outside the bar, the final stragglers lingered, smoking cigarettes, talking, cruising, making their final choice of the evening. Someone long ago had dubbed it sidewalk sale. Generally, it was finished by the time I walked out and locked the doors.

That night as I left, there were two or three guys hanging around out front and a couple more in a parked car. I locked the door and started to walk home. I always walked home. It was about six blocks, and with parking as bad as it was it didn't make sense to drive. On the weekend I might not find a space closer than six blocks anyway, and I definitely wouldn't find a spot near my house at three in the morning.

Most nights it was a lovely walk: the air fresher than it had been during the day, the streets empty, the city quiet in a way it almost never was. On my way, I walked by a little park that had been, at some point, cruisy. There were signs that said you couldn't drive past the same spot more than twice. Every so often, I'd see someone trying to score, staring at the few cars that went by.

On the far side, there was an open stage where there would occasionally be a musical performance or, sometimes, a little free Shakespeare. As I walked by, two guys came out from behind it. I assumed they'd been having sex back there; they were moving slowly and a bit furtively. They looked familiar. Were they the guys I'd noticed in the parked car? Had they been in the bar earlier?

And then they were close to me. Too close. They were both in their thirties, stocky, muscled, hair-trimmed close—military almost. One of the guys hooked my ankle, his foot pulling me down. I took a few dancing steps before I landed on the sidewalk face first. I tried getting up, but the two of them were on me, kicking me in the side and ribs. They called me a faggot a couple of times, putting me on familiar territory. I'd been to this rodeo before.

I lay on my side, my arms held up in front of my head, my knees protecting my belly. They'd get bored in a minute and go away, I told myself. And they did stop after a bit. Except for their heavy breathing, they were quiet. Then one of them, I didn't see which, leaned down close to me and said, "Learn to mind your own business, faggot."

And that's when I knew this wasn't about me being gay. This was about Danny Osborne. I could hear them walking away. I pulled myself up off the sidewalk. They were about twenty feet away by then, walking slowly as though they didn't have a care in the world. I bolted down the street after them.

I don't know why. I certainly didn't think it through, but a few seconds later I flew into one of them, the shorter one, and we went down. Quickly, I got myself up again and planted a foot smack in the center of the one guy's back. The other was coming at me, so I stole his move and kicked him in the ankle, knocking him off balance.

"Who are you?" I yelled. "Who the fuck are you!"

In a moment, I was tackled. Back on the ground. Kicked square in the stomach. I puked a little.

"Come on, let's get out of here," one of them said.

"In a minute," the other replied. Then he spit on me. They both spit on me.

I listened to them walk away and lay there a long while. Finally, I stood up and walked home. When I got there, I sat on the front stoop for a long time. The lights were out. Nobody was awake. I knew I needed to go in and wake Ronnie up. I might need to go to the emergency room, I wasn't sure. I was sure I didn't want to.

"Oh my God, what happened to you?" Ronnie asked when I woke him.

"It's not a big deal."

"You got bashed," he said. "I knew you shouldn't walk home in the middle of the night."

"I've done it hundreds of times. This has only happened once."

I decided to let him think I'd been bashed. I didn't want him to know it was related to the job he'd wanted me to take. For one thing, he'd feel guilty. For another, he might want me to stop.

"Oh Dom! This is terrible."

"I don't mean to intrude," Junior said, sticking his head into the bedroom. "But I couldn't help overhearing." Then he opened the door enough to let light in from the hallway. "Oh my. We need to get you cleaned up. Come use this bathroom."

The original bathroom was large, with built-in vanities, a shower *and* a bathtub. As I've said, our bathroom had once been a closet—a large closet but still a closet. I didn't know how Junior knew so much about our house after only a few days—did he wander around while we were out?

We went down to the big bathroom. All the lights were on, making me squint. Well, as best I could. One eye was kind of swollen. Junior sat me on the edge of the tub. He wore a paisley robe over striped pajamas. Ronnie hovered behind him in a pair of silk boxers.

"Darling, is your nose broken?" Junior asked.

"Not any more than it was this morning."

"Dom, now that you're working with Lydia, maybe you should stop working at The Hawk. You really don't need to."

I felt a sharp pang of guilt—or maybe I'd broken a rib, I wasn't sure. "I'll just drive from now on."

"You still have to walk to the car."

"We used to have patrols," Junior said. "This kind of thing happened all the time, so we organized patrols to keep people safe."

I didn't know why he was talking like it was ancient history. They'd done something like that when I was bartending up in Silver Lake.

Junior had rinsed out a washrag and begun dabbing my forehead. "The leather boys loved patrolling. Of course, most of them thought all they had to do was walk around and it would scare people off."

"I'm going to come and get you," Ronnie said. "When you're done you can call me, and I'll come get you."

"I could call a cab."

"You've got a really bad gash here. I think you should have stitches."

"And an X-ray," Ronnie added. "He could have a head injury."

"Did you get punched in the stomach?" Junior asked.

"A little."

"He could have internal injuries. Go get dressed, dear," he said to Ronnie. To me he said, "I really did think I'd live to see the day when this kind of thing stopped happening. You'll call the rags, won't you?"

"No. I don't want to see this in *Frontiers*."

"Oh but—" he stopped himself. "I'm sorry. Of course, you can deal with this however you think best."

"I don't want anyone to know."

INTERLUDE

August 27, 1984

It was the first day of school, a couple of weeks since Dix and Piglet had last seen each other. They were leaning up against the back of Piglet's red Datsun Z smoking Marlboro Lights.

"They arrested Duncan's brother," Piglet said.

"Yeah, I know, man. Don't talk about it, okay?"

"I'm not talking about it to anybody but you."

"Don't talk about it with me. I don't want to talk about it."

"We did something bad, something we can't undo. Why don't you wanna talk about it?"

"Forget about it. Don't think about it. Don't talk about it."

"But you do think about it, don't you?"

Dix got a funny look on his face, and said, "Yeah, I think about it. I think about it a lot."

They smoked a moment, then crushed out their cigarettes. "Gimme another," Piglet said.

"The bell's gonna ring."

"Are you sorry?"

"What?"

"Are you sorry about what we did?"

"No," Dix told him. "And don't you be sorry either."

"I can't help it. Don't you remember the look on her face? She just gave up. She was gone before she was gone."

"What good is that doing? We did what we did. Forget about it."

"Yeah, but can't I be sorry? Can't you—"

Dix punched him in the shoulder. "Shut up. Just shut up."

"I don't want to shut—"

Dix punched him again, this time square in the center of his chest. He fell to the ground and then scrambled back up.

"Is this what you're going to be like?" Dix asked. "Whining all the time? Cause I can't take it. You hear me, I can't."

"It's not wrong to feel sorry."

"It is. Because first you want to tell me you're sorry, but that won't be enough. You're going to have to tell someone else how sorry you are and that's where it's going to get bad, you see? You need to learn to shut your mouth. And you need to stay away from me."

"But you're my best friend."

"Stay away from me."

"Dix—"

"You don't stay away from me, I'll make you sorry. You hear me? You say anything I'll make you sorry!"

"You don't mean that."

"What we did to that girl, that's nothing compared to what I'll do to you if you don't keep your mouth shut and stay the fuck away from me."

The bell rang. It was time to start their senior year.

FIFTEEN

February 19, 1996
Monday morning

I stayed home most of that weekend. Partly because Ronnie didn't want me going anywhere, anywhere at all, and partly because John Gallagher had scrounged up a dozen Oxycontin. An opiate vacay seemed in order. By Monday morning, there was only one pill left.

As I came out of my stupor of pain and pain pills on Sunday night, I began putting things together. Someone wanted me to stop what I was doing. Someone wanted Danny to stay in prison. Well, of course they did. As long as he was there, no one was looking for the real killer. So I might have been beaten-up by the real killers. Or I might have been beaten-up by someone they hired—wait a minute. Had I met Dix and Piglet? Were they the ones who kicked the crap out of me? I couldn't think of any reason to think they were or any reason to think they weren't.

Were they the only possibilities? Waterstone might have had me jumped to avoid looking bad. That was a stretch. No, Waterstone wouldn't have. He was a lawyer and thought most things could be solved with a carefully written motion. The same for Piper. He had the power of the state on his side. He didn't need to have me beat-up. That left Montero. He'd certainly screwed the case up. But then, he seemed to have been screwing up cases all along, so why worry about this one? As the evening wore on and the Oxycontin wore off, I became more and more convinced I'd had a run in with Dix and Piglet.

"You're not going anywhere," Ronnie said on Monday morning when I got out of bed to get ready for work.

"I don't feel that bad. Honest." The gash on my forehead had begun to itch. I could almost take a full breath without feeling like I was re-fracturing my ribs. The bruise on my belly was tender but had already turned deep purple and red with a few yellow highlights at the edges.

"Lydia will be fine without you."

"I know. Ronnie, I like what I'm doing and I want to go to work."

He tried not to look too happy about that. "Okay, but just half a day."

"I promise I'll come home if I feel too bad."

He scowled. "That means you're staying all day."

"Ronnie—"

"Dom," he said, making fun of my tone.

"Do you have clients this afternoon?"

"Yes, two. But I'll be finished by four."

"Then I'll come home at four."

"Don't be like that."

There wasn't much else for him to say. He wasn't going to cancel clients—not that I wanted him to. "All right. I mean, it's not like you'll be in any danger."

And that, of course, was where he was wrong. I'd decided to go back to Happy Acres before I went into the office. I wanted to talk to Larry Tribble again. Or Not-Larry Tribble. Whoever he was.

I took a shower. My first without help. My scrapes had scabbed over, so it wasn't too painful. I did have a little trouble lifting my arms up to shampoo my hair. Other than a few bruises my arms were fine—it was my ribs that really didn't like that position. I pulled on my jeans, buttoned them, and then opted for a pink Oxford shirt Ronnie had gotten me one time. I never wore it, but it didn't have to go over my head. An old pair of penny loafers alleviated the need to bend over and tie my shoes.

Ronnie made me a breakfast of oatmeal—he'd read somewhere it was good for lowering cholesterol. For some reason he wanted to keep me alive. I ate most of it, promising myself I could stop for an egg and sausage biscuit. Hey, I was healing. I needed to keep up my strength.

Trying to find a subject other than me, Ronnie looked up from the morning's newspaper, and said, "Buchanan is doing really well in the primaries."

"He's a wacko," I pointed out.

"A dangerous wacko."

It was a strange world. Ronnie was born after Bobby Kennedy's assassination. I could remember his brother's presidency. The hope they inspired, the hope Martin Luther King inspired, that was gone. Instead, we'd turned inward, watching our bank accounts and judging each other by our wardrobes. And yet people like Ronnie and me, we had it better now than we'd ever had it before. The sixties and seventies were terrible for us. And then, even with AIDS, even with Reagan, things got better. We had lives, relationships, businesses, jobs, commitment ceremonies. It was better.

I should have probably talked about that with Ronnie, but I didn't. He kissed me and went off to his office. He had listings to pull and a dozen other things to take up his day. I should have asked him about the situation with his mother. I was sure she'd been calling.

There were biscuit crumbs all down the front of me when I pulled into Happy Acres for the second time in a week. I found Larry Tribble's pink trailer and parked. I brushed myself off, threw the McDonald's bag into the back and got out of the Jeep. A minute later, I knocked on Larry's door and he was there in a flash.

"Well, well. I can only think of one reason for you to come back so soon—I hope this isn't disappointing, but I'm a lady. You'll have to buy me dinner first."

I decided to play along. "I have to say, it would be the first time I ever dated a dead man."

"I know I'm a little pale but I'd hardly—" The look on my face stopped him. It was clearly dawning on him that I wasn't going to fall for charming little evasions. "Well, I suppose you should come inside."

He held the door open and I slipped through. We sat down in the kitchen again. Exactly the same spots as before.

"Have you told anyone I was here the other day?"

"Good God no. Why would I do that?" He squinted at me. "Oh my. Someone rearranged your features. You look like a Picasso."

"You should see my belly. It's even more abstract."

I could see that he wanted to say something dirty but was resisting the temptation. "So, what *do* you want?"

"Piglet's real name."

"I don't know his real name. I told you."

"I think you do."

He shrugged and said, "Well, I don't."

"Do you know your own name?" I asked, knowing the answer. "Leonard?"

"I changed my name. Big deal. People around here still call me Larry. It's nothing."

"You're still getting your brother's disability checks, are they nothing?"

"Look, you don't have any idea what it was like. I'd been doing drugs for ages. I had HIV, I had Hep C, I had a bunch of other things. I called myself the alphabet boy. Then my brother died, suddenly, at home, and I just told everyone he was me. It was kind of shocking. They barely checked. Out of respect, I suppose."

He sighed heavily, then said, "I should have offered you tea or something. There's no alcohol, of course."

"I'm fine."

"Water? I mean, it's the least I can do since you've come all this way to blackmail me."

"Sure, I'll have a glass of water."

He went to the sink and poured a glass. When he set it down in front of me, he continued. "Anyway, I didn't think I'd be cashing Leonard's checks for long. I didn't think I was long for this world, after all. But then —I got sober. I don't have one of those horrific hitting bottom stories. Like, literally finding myself in a gutter. No, I got up one morning and thought how boring it was being an addict. I mean, every day's basically the same. I had to scrape together some money, then I had to score some dope, then I had to take it. And then I had to do it all again. So, five years ago, I said fuck it and went to NA."

He sighed again. "And here you are. Ready to ruin it all."

"I don't have to ruin anything. You could tell me Piglet's real name."

"But then I'd end up dead. And, I don't know, death has always seemed kind of boring as well. Something I'd like to avoid."

"Nobody has to know you told me."

"You're here. They know."

"Who are they? And how do they know?"

"Well, you've met them, obviously. And I'd guess it was Peggy who dropped a dime on you."

That made sense to me. She was the one who'd lied to me the most. I took a sip of the water and sat there. My gut said he was going to give me Piglet's real name. I just had to be patient. I stared at him. He stared at me.

"You know, I miss my brother. I do. It's nice seeing his name on a check every month." He sighed heavily, yet again, and said, "Aaron Angler."

"You're sure?"

"Of course, I'm sure."

I hadn't heard the name before. It was new to me. Somehow, I thought it might be someone on the list Danny had given me. But that was wrong, I should have seen it. Danny didn't know Piglet's real name. The names he gave me, he knew those people.

"How is it you know Piglet's real name but Danny didn't?"

"We all went to school together. Aaron and I were a year ahead of Danny. Every time he saw me in the hallway, Aaron would call me a fag. You remember people like that, don't you? Or at least I do. Maybe he never called Danny a fag. Maybe it wasn't the kind of thing Danny even noticed."

"What about Dix? Do you know his real name?"

"I remember him. He transferred in for senior year. I don't remember his name. I was already using."

As I left, Larry made a point of asking me not to come back. I promised I wouldn't, though I might have been lying. Before I left the trailer park, I stopped by Peggy McCallister's trailer and banged on the door for a while. Her car was in the driveway and I saw her peek out to see who was there—but she wouldn't open the door.

That confirmed it. She was the one who'd gotten me beaten up. Charming.

———

I was back in Long Beach walking into the Freedom Agenda office about a half an hour later. Karen took one look at me and asked, "What happened to you?"

"I fell down a flight of stairs."

"That's what she said."

"Trust me. My boyfriend didn't beat me up."

"Mmmm-hmmm. She said that too."

"Is Lydia here?"

"She was. She had to meet a painter at her house. She left a message for you, though." There were papers scattered around her desk, but she knew exactly where to reach for the note. "There's a name on Waterstone's witness list. He wasn't called during the trial. She wants to figure out what he was supposed to testify to and why he didn't."

"What's the name?"

"Aaron Angler."

Every hair on my body stood up. "Aaron Angler?"

"Yes. That's what I said." She looked at me suspiciously.

"He's Piglet."

"Piglet?"

"He's around Danny's age. He and a friend were hanging around Duncan's buying drugs. They're the ones who left with Audrey. They're the ones who might have killed her."

She narrowed her eyes at me, "Why's he called Piglet?"

"His father was a cop."

"Uh-uh," she said, shaking her head. She flipped through a couple of folders and then handed one to me. "Aaron Angler's father worked at Boeing."

"Okay."

"He's also dead."

"His father?"

"No, Aaron."

SIXTEEN

February 19, 1996
Monday afternoon

I was tempted to ask Karen if it was common to end up with a lot of dead witnesses, but I realized that was a stupid question. The case was more than a decade old and revolved around drug addicts. Of course there would be a lot of dead witnesses.

I took the file to the back, sat down in my brand new, lumbar-supporting chair—which was even more important than it had been on Friday. Next to me, on the overcrowded banquet table, was a ragtag pile of files and paperwork which, together, constituted what I'd been given on the Osborne case so far. I looked through the file Karen had put together on Aaron Angler.

Born April 1, 1966 to a Deborah and Todd Angler. He would have been almost thirty. He graduated from Westmoreland High School class of 1985. He attended Orange County Community College for a year and a half year. After that, he was in the army until 1990 when he was dishonorably discharged. His obituary appeared in *The Orange County Register* in November of 1992. Not surprisingly, he died of a drug overdose.

So why did Larry Tribble think Aaron's father was a policeman? Was there another reason his nickname was Piglet? Had he actually been fat? Or even a little chubby? Was he an obnoxious, chubby hall monitor in high school?

It wasn't making sense. In the file, there were a couple of addresses for him. The first was 8809 Emerald Avenue in Westmoreland, the second 502 E. Sycamore in Anaheim, and the last was 5535 Via Santiago back in Westmoreland. Something seemed familiar about all of this, but I wasn't sure what it was. I grew up near an Emerald Avenue. That was probably it. Street names were often the same from town to town. Most places had a Broadway or a Main. People have never been especially creative.

Setting Aaron's file aside, I flipped through my mess until I found my copy of Waterstone's case file. I flipped through until I found the witness list. Karen was right. Aaron Angler was on it. His was the final name.

Waterstone had known about Piglet and Dix. He'd planned to call Piglet. But he didn't. Why? And how had he convinced Angler to get on the stand? If he and Dix were the ones who killed the girl, why would he testify?

The bell rang at the front meaning the front door was opened. I heard Lydia say good morning to Karen and something else I couldn't hear. Then, Karen said, "He's in the back." Lydia was looking for me. Good, I had plenty to tell her.

She didn't even take off her thin overcoat or drop her purse in her office. Just came straight back to see me. After giving me a good long scowl, she said, "Ronnie tells me you got bashed."

I shrugged. "It happens."

"Bullshit."

"You don't think gays get beat up in the street anymore?"

"I'm sure they do. I just don't think it happened to you."

"Why is that?"

"It's too coincidental. You interview some potential witnesses in Danny's case and then you get beat-up. It doesn't make sense that there wouldn't be a connection."

"How was the painter?"

"Awful. Don't change the subject."

"Why was he awful?"

"Because he didn't listen to me," she said, pointedly. "Look, if your getting beat-up had something to do with Danny's case you have to tell me."

"And if it does have to do with the case you can't tell Ronnie."

"But—" she began, then changed her demeanor. "Did they say anything to you?"

"That I should mind my own business."

"That's it?"

"Seemed like enough at the time."

"Ronnie said you don't want to go to the police. Do you think that's wise?"

"I don't know. Maybe, maybe not."

"I'm sorry I put you in harm's way. Just work in the office this week. Do you have health insurance?"

"Don't worry about it."

"We'll cover your medical costs."

I glanced at the stacks and stacks of files on the long table. If I let her pay my medical bills a couple people would stay in prison that much longer because she couldn't test their DNA.

I shook my head. "Call it a donation."

"We'll talk about it later."

We wouldn't, if I could avoid it. I moved on, "Aaron Angler."

"Oh yes. His name was on Waterstone's witness list but he didn't testify. We need to find out everything about him so I can depose him."

"He's dead. Karen found his obituary."

"Shit."

"And... he's Piglet."

"Gut feeling?"

"No, I went down to Happy Acres this morning and talked to Larry Tribble. He said Aaron Angler is Piglet."

"He suddenly remembered that?"

"He did."

She didn't want to know more than that. Ethically, if she knew of an ongoing crime she was legally bound to report it. The fact that Larry wasn't her client might change that, but a discussion of the finer points wouldn't help anyone.

"Just one problem," I continued. "Larry says Piglet's father was a cop. But Aaron Angler's father worked at Boeing."

"So, he's *not* Piglet."

"I don't know. Haven't figured it out yet."

"Will Tribble testify?"

"Not willingly," I said. It would likely expose him, since the first thing he'd have to do is state his name.

"Well, keep on it," Lydia said.

"From back here?"

"Yes, from back here. Use the telephone."

I spent the rest of the morning reading through the trial transcript. What interested me most was the very ending of the defense. After the final witness, the judge asked if Waterstone would like to call any more witnesses.

"One moment, your honor," he said. There must have been a long pause, or perhaps he was consulting with Danny, because the judge said, "Counselor?"

"No, your honor, the defense rests."

What transpired in-between, "One moment, your honor," and "Counselor?" It had to have been at least a minute, possibly more. Was Waterstone just sitting there or was he talking to Danny? Or was he talking to someone else?

Unfortunately, a transcript is just a record of what's said, little more. You don't get to look at the players and try to figure out if they're lying. Or if they're only telling part of the truth. So why wasn't Aaron Angler called to the stand?

I flipped back through the defense's case. The final witness was William Peterson. He testified on the afternoon of February eleventh. That morning, Waterstone was late for court about fifteen minutes. The judge scolded him and asked if he'd like to call any more witnesses. The curious exchange then followed.

Had something happened on the night of February tenth? Waterstone could have rested his case that afternoon, but he didn't. So the question was, why?

Of course, the answer was simple. It was as plain as the bruises on my face. Someone had threatened him. I wondered how to confirm that. I got up and went out to see Karen. She was on the phone. Looking up at me, she said into the receiver, "Denise? I'm gonna need to call you back." She hung up and gave me the eye. "You want something. What is it?"

"Is there a way to look at police reports? In particular, the week of February fourth through tenth 1985."

"Do you have a name?"

"Waterstone, possibly."

She frowned at me. "Colin Waterstone?"

"Yes."

"Police records are not public."

I knew that, of course. I was hoping she had a way around it.

"I could try the California Public Records Act, but that will take a while and they usually deny them at least once. What are you looking for?"

"I want to know if he reported any threats or violent acts during that time period."

"During the trial? He should have reported that to the judge."

"Absolutely. But if he believed the threat he might not have."

Karen shrugged and said, "I'll see what I can find."

I left the front and stood in Lydia's open doorway. She was on the phone, "I promise I'll find a painter soon. Just not this one." I stepped back to give her privacy, but she waved me in. "Because he was pushy and obnoxious. All he wanted to do was sell me on his color ideas. He must have a ton of 'snow-capped white' and 'powder blue sky' that he's trying to get rid of."

She listened for a moment or two. "I promise, I will take care of it. I have to go into a meeting right now. I love you, too."

Hanging up the phone, she rolled her eyes. "We have about ten days to get the house painted. He's going to be pissy right up until the minute we move in. What can I do for you?"

"I have a hunch."

"Do you?"

"I think Waterstone knew Aaron Angler was Piglet. I think he's the reason they were offered such a great deal, and when Danny turned it down they managed to scare Waterstone enough that he didn't call him."

"If Waterstone knew who Piglet was, why didn't Danny?"

That stumped me. It just made sense that if Waterstone was calling Aaron Angler to say he was Piglet that Danny was the one who'd given him that information. And if Danny hadn't told him, who had and why didn't Waterstone tell Danny? Okay, the second half of that I knew the answer to. Waterstone only saw Danny three times. Then I remembered something else.

"One thing," I said. "Danny said he didn't go to high school with either Dix or Piglet. Larry Tribble said Aaron Angler went to school with them. And that Dix transferred at the beginning of senior year."

Lydia supplied the rest. "But Danny also said he barely went to school. Maybe they were there, and he just didn't know it."

"But if they went through all of school together, even if they were a couple of years a part, he'd know Piglet, at least. From when he did go to school."

Lydia nodded, but said, "Not everything fits together, Dom. There are always things that appear to contradict."

I didn't like that answer. I wanted things to fit. To make sense.

"I have two big questions," I said. "One: Who told Waterstone about Aaron Angler in the first place? And two: Why didn't he have him testify?"

"This might help," Karen said, placing herself on the other side of Lydia's doorway. She handed me a printout from her computer. It was a very brief article from *The Orange County Register*. I read it aloud:

COSTA MESA—A fire broke out at a home on Valencia Court in Costa Mesa Sunday morning about three a.m. Three fire trucks were called to the scene and quickly extinguished the fire. No one at the home was injured. Damage is estimated to be around fifty thousand dollars. Arson is suspected.

"Okay. Why is this important?" I asked.

Karen handed me another sheet, saying, "In 1985, Waterstone lived on Valencia Court."

"Good work, Karen," Lydia said.

"He could be disbarred, couldn't he?"

"We can't prove anything, so no."

"But if he was threatened, he had to know Danny was innocent."

"Danny is a drug addict," Karen said. "Going to prison may have saved his life."

"You don't really think—"

The bell at the front rang and Ronnie's voice followed, "Hello! I have pizza!"

I hadn't realized it, but it was lunch time. Of course, this was Ronnie's way of checking up on me, making sure I was getting through my first day of complete mobility okay.

We went out into the reception area. There were a couple of ancient office chairs—nearly as uncomfortable as the folding chair I'd sat on my first few days.

When he saw me, he said, "I brought your favorite. Chicken pesto from The Pizza Place." In other words, he knew this might not go over well.

"Thank you," I said. "Did you bring enough for everyone?"

"It's a large."

"Put it on my desk, I'll get some napkins," Karen said, and went back to the coffee station for napkins.

"Did you see what they did to my boyfriend?" Ronnie said to Lydia.

"I did. He seems to be recovering though."

"I want him to go to the police, but he refuses."

"Well, sometimes the police are more trouble than they're worth," Lydia said, looking awkward.

"That's not fair," Ronnie said. "You're *my* friend. You should be on my side."

"Things like this are too important for sides," Lydia said. Then, desperate to change the subject, she asked, "Do you have any painters you can recommend?"

Of course he did, so they talked about painters for a bit. Karen came back and handed out slices of pizza on large dinner napkins. We all agreed the pizza was delicious. Ronnie made small talk, wanting to know if any of us had seen the previews for *The Birdcage*.

"I haven't," Lydia said.

"Totally cliched," he announced. "Looks to be full of horrific stereotypes. I can't wait to see it."

"Interesting recommendation," Karen said.

"Dwayne says Robin Williams is a genius but quite the handful," Lydia said. "The pizza's wonderful by the way."

"Isn't it?" Ronnie said, then turned to me. "How do you feel?"

"I'm fine. Just like I was three hours ago."

"He won't tell you," he said to Lydia. "But if it looks like he's in pain send him home."

"Of course."

"Promise?"

"Promise."

SEVENTEEN

February 19, 1996
Monday evening

I did leave early but not because I was in pain. Not that I wasn't in pain—I was. I just wasn't going to let that stop me. I took Atlantic up to 7th and then cut across town to the San Diego Freeway. Big mistake. It was rush hour. Somewhere in front of me there was a SigAlert. No one ever talked about it, but I suspected most Southern Californians had a deep and abiding fear of becoming a SigAlert.

My cellular phone rang. I jumped. It was Ronnie.

"I'm so, so sorry!"

"What for?" I asked.

"I got a new client this afternoon and I have to show them a bunch of houses. Tonight! I don't think I'll be home until after nine. Are you home yet?"

"Almost there," I lied.

"Good. You need to rest. I could bring home Star of Siam. Or should I have something delivered?"

"Thai is fine. I want the broccoli noodles with beef."

"Are you mad at me?" he asked.

"Why would I be mad at you?"

"For the pizza."

"I'm not mad at you, but you do need to stop."

"Yes, Daddy."

"Grrrrrr…"

He knew I hated being called Daddy. The gap in our ages was better ignored. He laughed and said goodbye.

Traffic was slow, until Fountain Valley when I reached the SigAlert. A catering van had tangled with the guardrail and flipped over. Crudité covered two lanes. I was wondering what kind of event they were going to on a Monday night—and obviously weren't going to make—when I got off the freeway in Costa Mesa. Using my *Thomas Guide*, I made my way to Valencia Court.

It was a cul-de-sac with five houses. Modest homes. Or at least they'd begun that way. No one with a modest income could afford them—even though prices were still somewhat depressed from the Northridge quake.

No, in other parts of the world the people who lived on Valencia Court would have much more impressive homes. Instead, they lived in ranch houses, lavished attention on their landscaping, and spent their extra cash on thirty thousand-dollar SUVs. Well, almost everyone. One of the houses was not freshly painted or landscaped or in anyway remarkable. In its driveway sat a Toyota Corolla from the eighties. I suspected they'd been there a while, and that was exactly what I was looking to find.

I parked in front of the house and got out of my Jeep. I walked up the scorched driveway and across a concrete walkway to the front door. The door had a four-paned window. In the lower right pane was a sign for ADT security. Based on the condition of the house, I guessed they didn't have ADT anymore—if they'd ever had it. ADT signs were much more common than actual customers.

I pulled open the screen door and knocked on the door. Then I noticed there was a doorbell. Oh, well.

A woman in her seventies moved the curtains on the door and looked out at me. "What do you want?"

"Hi. I'd like to ask a few questions about a fire that happened a few years ago."

"Why?"

Briefly, I debated which would work better: the truth or a lie. I went with a lie. "I'm from the insurance company."

She opened the door a few inches. The chain prevented it from opening further. "You're lying. That claim was paid years ago."

"Yeah, well, we've had some trouble with an adjuster. She was submitting fraudulent claims and we're having to go back and check all her work. You might have seen something about it on the news."

"Maybe I did."

"Anyway. Did you live here in 1985?"

"I've lived here since 1962."

"Good. Now, which house was it that had a fire that year?"

"Right next door."

I looked over at the pretty blue ranch house next door. I noticed that the windows on the side were similar but not exactly the same as the windows on the front.

"That was the Waterstone's, right?"

"Uh-huh. She was a pretty little thing. We didn't see him much though. Work-a-holic." The way she'd said workaholic put it right up there with drug dealer or prostitute.

"Can you tell me what you remember about the fire?"

"Don't you have a report?"

"Yes, of course, but we don't know if it's accurate. That's why I'm here."

"It was one of them homemade mazel tov cocktails. Little red sports car came barreling in and somebody threw it out the window."

"Did you see it happen?"

"Of course, I saw it happen. I was sitting right where you're standing."

"Did you see the person who threw the... homemade bomb?" I didn't want to say Molotov cocktail since it might sound like I was correcting her.

"Teenager. It's always teenagers."

"Boy?"

"Yeah. Seventeen, eighteen. White—that surprised me. But then they integrated the schools, so what do you expect?"

"Did you hear anything about why the Waterstone's were targeted?"

"He was a public defender back then. You know the kind of scum he had to work with. Probably one of them."

"They don't still live there, do they?"

"Oh no. They left—God, the house had barely been put back together when they had a for sale sign up. And he got on at some big firm. Moved up in the world."

I thought for a moment then doubled back. "When you say the fire had something to do with his work, that's just a guess? You didn't actually hear anything?"

"No. It's not a guess. His wife said something to me."

"Did she? Do you remember what she said?"

She exhaled like I'd asked her something truly ridiculous. "Well, let's see. She'd come over every so often and have coffee and a muffin. I like to bake, you see. And there's just me. Sometimes I'd call her up and ask her over. So this one time, right after the fire—" When she'd purposely baked so she'd have an excuse to invite the woman over, I assumed. "—she said her husband was scared after it happened. He told her how much he loved her and that he was going to do something for her, but she didn't really know what that was."

I knew. I knew exactly what it was.

———

I was looking forward to a nice quiet evening. Possibly even sitting with a single glass of wine ruminating about everything I'd learned. And then having a late dinner. Waterstone knew who Aaron Angler was and didn't put him on the stand because he was afraid. That meant someone was protecting Aaron Angler. His father. A cop. Except his father wasn't a cop. Of course, it might be Dix who was being protected. And Piglet who was ready to spill the beans.

I should probably talk to Aaron Angler's mother. She would know who Aaron's friends were. She would know who Dix was. Hopefully, he was still alive.

When I walked into my kitchen, my plan for a quiet evening went out the window. Mai Chen was sitting at the counter with Junior. Neither looked happy.

"Would you like a glass of wine, Mai?" I asked.

"I already offered her one," Junior said, which made me bristle a bit. He'd only been here a couple of days and he was already acting the host.

"I'd like to see Ronnie," Mai said.

"He's showing houses tonight. I don't think he'll be home until late."

I went to the refrigerator and took out a bottle of white. It was Trader Joe's but one of their better brands. I poured a glass and set one in front of Mai. I didn't offer anything to Junior, hoping he'd take the hint. He didn't.

Mai sipped the wine without saying thank you. She looked lovely. Her hair was perfect, her deep blue outfit well-tailored and crisp. The only indication I could see that she was upset was her foundation clumping around the frown lines between her eyebrows.

"Dom, tell us about your job. It sounds so exciting," Junior said brightly. I gave him a look which he finally read correctly. "Oh, you know, on second thought, I think I'll go upstairs to my room. I have things to do, letters to write."

I waited until he left the room and then I waited some more. Mai had finished three quarters of her wine. I poured her some more.

"A child should honor his parents," she finally said. "Don't you agree?"

"Not really. I've seen parents do terrible things to their children. They shouldn't be honored for that."

"You think I'm a bad mother."

"I didn't say that. You want what's best for you son."

"Then you understand."

"You want to *decide* what's best for your son. That's different."

That earned me a glare. I was grateful I didn't get the glass of wine thrown in my face.

"Mai, you could lose him completely."

"You want to take him away from me."

"You probably won't believe this, but I'm on your side."

"Then you will help. He needs a wife." She blushed a bit as she said, "It doesn't have to be a large change. And she would be helpful. To both of you."

"Wouldn't that be kind of awful for the girl?"

"I don't think so. You have no idea what these girls come from."

What a terrible thought. That a girl could be so desperate that marrying a gay man, and living with him and his lover as little more than a maid would be acceptable.

"I think it would be awful."

"You're an American. You have no sense of duty."

"Ronnie's an American. And so are you."

She looked puzzled for a moment. She spoke fluent French because her family had been prominent when Viet Nam was ruled by the French. She was Chinese but had never lived there. She was Vietnamese though she really didn't want to be. And she *was* American, just as I'd said.

Standing, she said, "I think I've taken enough of your time." She started out and I followed her.

On the front stoop, I said, "I hope I see you soon, Mai."

Shaking her head, she said, "No, I don't think so."

EIGHTEEN

February 20, 1996
Tuesday morning

I am not a cuddler; Ronnie is. He's learned that at some point during the night, I'm going to slip away from him and stake out my own space. He's also learned to deal with the dreams I sometimes have. The dreams which make me moan and whimper and cry out; that make me push him away before I'm fully awake. Dreams that once made me push him all the way out of the bed.

That next morning, he'd turned the alarm off, so I didn't wake up until I was a half an hour late for work. He'd made his way back to me and was wrapped around me like a python.

"Oh shit," I said when I saw the alarm. He rolled over and looked at it and joined me.

"Oh shit."

I grabbed my jeans from the day before and pulled a clean shirt out of the closet. I was going to have to forgo a shower and skip breakfast.

"I'll call Lydia and tell her it's my fault."

"You don't need to do that. It'll be fine."

Then I relaxed a little bit. I was late. It wasn't the end of the world. Lydia probably didn't even need me first thing.

"I'm so sorry," Ronnie said.

"It's fine," I said, bending over the bed and kissing him. He'd come in late from showing houses. I didn't tell him his mother had been there. Didn't tell him what she'd said. She deserved time to change her mind. And so did Ronnie.

We'd watched a little TV in bed and fallen asleep after *Letterman*—or during, I couldn't remember. Just before or just after midnight.

The good thing about being late was that I'd momentarily forgotten my aches and pains. It was close to ten when I walked into the office. Karen looked up at me and said, "She's not here yet."

"Oh, okay."

"She's also not a stickler for punctuality unless you're on the way to court."

"Thanks."

I went to the back, poured myself a cup of sludgy coffee, and sat down. I wanted to look at everything I had on Waterstone. I knew what had happened. Why he'd hung his own client out to dry. But I didn't know yet how to prove it.

I looked through my stack of files and paperwork, and didn't find one on Waterstone. I went back up front and asked, "Did you do a file on Colin Waterstone?"

"Yes," she studied me a moment. "Oh, you weren't here yet. Sorry."

"No problem."

She got up and stepped over to the row of file drawers behind her desk and opened it up. A moment later she pulled out the file. "I'll make a copy and bring it to you."

I must be coming up in the world. In the back, I sat down in the Staples desk chair and sipped my coffee. Karen brought me the file.

"What's going on?" she asked, which could explain the kindness. Lydia had never said not to share things with Karen, and I had the feeling my life would be a lot easier if I shared this information with her.

"The Aaron Angler kid. I think he and his friend killed Audrey. Waterstone was going to put him on the stand. I doubt he was going to confess, but simply admitting his nickname was Piglet would be enough to raise reasonable doubt."

"But he didn't testify," she said. She must have gotten through the transcript.

"No, Waterstone's house was firebombed the night before."

"So, he didn't call Aaron Angler to the stand."

"Nope, he didn't."

I opened the file and began to look through it.

"What are you looking for?"

"A neighbor said he told his wife he did it for her."

"His first wife or his second wife?"

I stared at her. "His wife in 1985."

"That would be his first wife."

"We need to find her."

When Lydia walked in the door, I was standing behind Karen as she skimmed through a couple of programs looking for Donna Waterstone, who might have reverted to her maiden name—which we had yet to find.

"I found a painter, thank God! He won't start until a week from Friday, but he at least listens to me." Lydia wore a dusty gray suit with a black turtleneck and pearls.

Karen went to get her a cup of coffee and I followed Lydia into her office. By the time I caught her up on Waterstone and Aaron Angler, Karen was there with the coffee.

"We should find and talk to Waterstone's first wife," I said.

She shook her head. "No. We should talk to Aaron's mother. Karen, could you find her info?" Karen stepped away. To me, Lydia said. "She has to know who Dix is. As soon as we have his name, we can set a conference with the district attorney."

"Do you want to see her today?"

"I can't. I have court this afternoon in downtown L.A. Why don't you call her and find out what you can?"

"I'd rather go see her."

"Why?"

"Because it's easier to tell if people are lying."

She sighed. She knew I was right. Then Karen came back.

"She lives in Seal Beach. Her name is Daly now. The address looks familiar. I think it's Leisure World."

I looked at Lydia and said, "No one's going to attack me at a retirement home.

Out in front of Leisure World, there's an open metal globe with pastel continents tacked on. It's reminiscent of the sculpture that greeted visitors at the 1964 World's Fair, except for the pastel part. I pulled into the giant complex and stopped at the guard house. I told him I was there to see Deborah Daly, 90G Twin Hills Road.

"Is she expecting you?"

"No. It's kind of a surprise."

"Residents usually call and leave a pass for their guests."

"I'll keep that in mind for next time."

"I need to call her. Do you want to give me your name?"

"She doesn't know me. Tell her I'm a friend of her son, Aaron."

He looked at me suspiciously, but he went back into the room and made the call. A few minutes later, he was back with a pass.

"Do you know where you're going?"

"Sure," I lied. As soon as I got around the corner, I was going to take out my *Thomas Guide*. Once I'd located Twin Hills Road, I took the two necessary turns and was basically there. I did note that there were no hills whatsoever, twin or otherwise.

The apartments were one-story, faced with decorative concrete blocks, and built facing each other in a long row, like a couple of houses that just went on and on. Between the buildings was a long sidewalk. I was looking for the number when I saw a woman standing in her doorway a few units down.

She looked too young to live there. She was probably only in her late fifties. Her hair not completely gray, her skin-tight, her figure decent if a bit on the thin side. I'd had lovers her age. It was hard to think of her as old.

"Hello," I called out as I walked up to her. "You're Deborah Daly? Previously Deborah Angler?"

"I am. You're not a friend of Aaron's," she said as I got close.

"I never meet him, no. I'm looking into the Audrey Gunderson murder. He was scheduled to testify but then didn't."

"I don't know anything about that," she said, in an unconvincing voice.

"Do you remember a friend of Aaron's with the nickname Dix?"

She looked like I'd kicked the air out of her. "You'd better come in," she said, then turned and went back into the unit.

I walked through the front door. The apartment was very neat with plastic on the furniture. I always thought people who put plastic on their furniture were more interested in the appearance of a life than having an actual life. It was like they couldn't bear the idea that something might go wrong.

"Excuse me," she said as she left the room.

I stood in the center of her living room feeling awkward. Under the plastic was a sofa and two uncomfortable looking chairs. There was a print on the wall that looked to be cardboard underneath—a sailboat on a rough sea. On the console television was a collection of photographs. Aaron's senior picture—he looked awkward and pimply, not at all like the murderer he probably was—a couple of school photos from the years before, some candids, one of Aaron and his mother at Disneyland, another of the two of them with a dark man I didn't recognize.

She came back into the room with a tray that held a jug of iced tea and a couple of glasses. After setting the tray on the coffee table, she poured me a glass.

"Why are you looking into that poor girl's murder?"

"I work with a lawyer representing Danny Osborne. DNA tests show that he couldn't have killed Audrey."

"Is he out of prison?"

"Not yet."

"Soon though?"

"Hopefully."

She sipped her iced tea. She wasn't asking me what this might have to do with her son. After a moment, she asked, "Have you ever loved a drug addict?"

"No."

"Aaron was a drug addict. My son. I lost him years before he died. I tried to get him back. Begged. Pleaded. Paid for rehab. Twice. Nothing helped. I even went to a shrink myself. I suppose that helped, he told me to let go."

"Did Aaron ever talk to you about Audrey's murder?"

She shook her head.

"But you know he had something to do with it?"

"His high school picture, we were at The Broadway buying a shirt and tie for him to wear in the picture when he was served a subpoena."

I glanced at the picture; his dress shirt had thin black lines through it, while the tie was striped diagonally. Of course his mother picked it out. I waited for her to say more.

"I tried to get him to tell me why he'd been called to testify in a murder trial. At first he said he didn't know. Then he said he was probably called to say that Danny was a nice kid. I didn't believe that either."

"Did it have to do with his friend Dix?"

"He wouldn't say, but that's crossed my mind over the years."

"So, you know Dix? You know who he is?"

"Yes. Emmanuel Richards."

The name didn't mean anything. It was kind of a letdown. I'd expected things to come together when I found out who Dix really was.

"So, the nickname is about his last name: Richards."

"Yes. The boys were friends for a long time. When they hit puberty it became a joke to call Manny 'Couple of Dicks' because of Richards. That got shortened to Dicks." She paused, sipped her tea and then said, "Something happened at the beginning of senior year. They had a falling out. Aaron would never tell me what it was about. It was something big, though. Aaron's problems got much worse after the friendship ended."

"What did you think of Dix?"

"That's the irony. I thought he was awful. I thought he was a terrible influence. When the friendship ended, I thought it was the best thing for my son. But then it wasn't. Not at all."

"Why was Aaron called Piglet?"

"His father," she said, then shook her head. "Stepfather, I mean. Aaron's father and I split when Aaron was around three. I remarried a couple of years later. It's hard to think of Todd— Anyway, Aaron's stepfather was a police officer. Kids in the neighborhood thought it was funny to call him Piglet. I always hated it."

"And he was named Daly."

"No, that's my most recent mistake. No, Aaron's stepfather was Samuel Montero."

NINETEEN

February 20, 1996
Tuesday afternoon

It was just after lunchtime, peak daytime hours. Even though it was going to cost a fortune, I called the Freedom Agenda on my cellular phone and asked Karen to put Lydia on.

"She had to go home. Some kind of family emergency."

I asked for the number of Lydia's cellular phone. I was about to hang up, but then I realized I had some business with Karen. I didn't want to tell her about Montero since I hadn't yet told Lydia. So I phrased what I wanted as a question: "Do we know how Montero got assigned to the case?"

"It's in the transcript," Karen said, impressing me with her memory for details. "Vance Piper asked about it at the beginning of his testimony."

Well, there you go. I shouldn't have been skipping direct testimony. "What did they say?" I asked.

"Hold on," I heard the clump of the phone on the desk, then some rustling of paper. The transcript was right there on the desk. I'd noted it when I walked by. She'd already gone through it, using Post-It flags to mark the different sections. I had the feeling she'd gone over the transcript with a set of colored markers, too.

"Found it," she said, coming back. "Okay. Piper asks, 'When were you assigned the case?' Montero answers, 'Two days after the body was found.' Piper, 'Is that normal?' Montero, 'It's not abnormal. The case was originally assigned to a detective. The Chief felt it required someone of a higher rank. That's why it was given to me.'"

"Thanks," I said. It seemed obvious to me that Montero had used his rank to maneuver his way onto the case.

"What?" Karen asked.

"I should tell Lydia first."

"Oh, all right, fine." Then after a moment she asked, "You went to see Deborah Daly. Oh, shit!"

The phone dropped to the desk again. A moment later she was back, "Emerald Avenue. A Debbie Williams lived with Montero at the Emerald Avenue address. Is that Deborah Daly?"

"Yeah, she said she was married to Montero. I don't know where the Williams comes in."

Had she been married to someone between Todd Angler and Samuel Montero? Or was Williams her maiden name?

"Damn it. Emerald Avenue. I should have caught that."

So should I. The address had sounded familiar. I'd known that. I'd just been wrong about why.

"Don't worry about it," I told Karen. "And don't tell Lydia I told you first."

"You didn't tell me first. I figured it out."

After I hung up, I tried Lydia on her cellular. It went to voicemail. I left a message but only said that she should call me. That I had some new information. I didn't say what it was or how important it was.

When I got off the 405 at 7th, I began wondering what I wanted to do next. I could go back to the office and read through some files. but after the excitement of figuring out that Montero was connected to Piglet that seemed awfully dull.

Impulsively, I pulled off 7th and into the CSULB campus. Passing a lawn sculpture of random white blocks, I drove along the back side of campus. It was one of the largest campuses in California—and the world. The sixties mod buildings were huddled together on a wide swath of lawn. I crept along behind buildings until I saw something that might pass as a parking place—as long as I stayed in the Jeep.

What did I want to do next? Find Dix. He was the one who killed Audrey and all we had to do was test his DNA to prove it. What did we know about Emmanuel Richards? I made a mental list:

- He graduated from Westmoreland High class of 1985.
- Deborah Angler said they were old friends, but he began at Westmoreland in their final year. So where else did he go to school and why did they already know each other?
- What was Emmanuel Richards doing now? Had he assaulted and/or killed other women?
- Had Richards been the one who beat me up? And, since Piglet was dead, who was his new partner in crime?

I got my *Thomas Guide* out from under the seat. I flipped through the pages until I found Westmoreland High School. I made my way back out to 7th and headed down to Westmoreland.

It wasn't hard to find the high school. It covered an entire city block —well, a Southern California city block, which is as large as a small city. I drove around it, until I found what looked like an entrance. I left my Jeep in an area designated for visitor parking and walked up to the administration building. I noted that there were at least six 'portable classrooms' aka trailers at the far end of a parking lot. This school was growing faster than the buildings could keep up. It was a stark contrast to my Catholic high school, which had been housed in one old, cramped building.

Just inside the door was a reception area. The receptionist was a woman about my age, who'd probably recently been gaining weight. Her dress, which was not out of style, was tight, nearly bursting.

I doubted she'd just hand me the information I wanted, so I decided to lie. "Hi," I said, pasting a big smile on my face. "I wonder if I could ask some questions about the school? Perhaps speak to an alum?"

I don't know why, maybe it was my smile, but she decided to flirt with me, "You're a little old for high school, aren't you?"

I chuckled. "My son. He's fifteen. My wife, my ex-wife, has him at a Catholic school and he's not taking to it."

"Which one?" she asked, and then when she saw my clueless look added, "Sacred Heart, Santa Maria or St. Hedwig? Or is he further out?"

"Oh, um, I'd rather not say. I think the education he's getting is dreadful."

"Santa Maria," she supplied.

"Well, I don't really want to start rumors. Is there someone here I can talk to?"

"You know, you should just bring your son in, let him see for himself."

"I mainly have him on weekends. You know, a family friend graduated from here about ten years ago. Manny Richards. You weren't here ten years ago, were you?"

"I was, but I don't remember a boy named Manny. But then, I think I was on maternity leave for a lot of that year. You know, let me see if Miss Wilkie is available. She's one of our assistant principals… and former students. She should be able to answer your questions."

She wrote out a hall pass for me, which seemed ridiculous since I was clearly an adult, and pointed me down a hallway. "Third door on the left."

The hallway, indeed the entire building, was made of thickly painted cinderblock walls, buffed linoleum flooring and acoustic tiles on the ceiling. Inexpensive and nearly indestructible. When I got to the third door on the left, I knocked on the wooden door with a sliver of a window. I watched as a young woman rose from her desk and came to the door. She was thin, wispy-haired, and looked far too young to be an assistant principal. In fact, she seemed far too young to be anything.

It hit me that everyone involved with Audrey's death was far too young. Danny was still in his twenties and in prison, Aaron had died in his twenties, Audrey would be twenty-six if she'd—

"Can I help you?" she asked as she opened the door.

"Hi, I wonder if I could ask a few questions. I'm considering transferring my son here. The woman at the desk sent me—"

"Certainly, come in and have a seat."

She backed up and I entered the office. Letting the door fall behind her, she returned to her desk.

"I'm Amy Wilkie, vice principal."

"I'm Dom Reilly."

"Dom is an interesting name."

"Short for Dominick."

"From the Latin Dominicus. I think it means beloved of God."

"You have a good memory."

She shook her head. "Not really. I went through a Catholic phase, much to the dismay of my Episcopalian family. I tried to memorize all the saints, but then I found out there are thousands. Anyway, tell me about your son."

Since I had no son, I changed the direction of the conversation, "A family friend recommended the school. Do you happen to know Manny Richards?"

She stared at me. Her breathing quickened noticeably. Tightly, she said, "That's a lie. He's not a family friend of yours. Who are you?"

I was completely at a loss. My ruse had completely failed, so I reverted to the truth. "Do you remember Danny Osborne?"

"Yes, everyone does. Why are you asking about these boys? You don't have a son at all, do you?"

"I work for Danny's attorney. A DNA test shows that Danny couldn't have killed Audrey Gunderson. I'm—"

"You think Manny Richards killed her?"

"Yes, I do."

She sat still for a long moment. I was about to ask if she knew Audrey, if that was why she was upset, but then she began to speak.

"I went to CSULB. It's a good teaching college. My best friend was MaryBeth Park. She was pretty, petite, Korean-American—gorgeous black hair. Born in Cerritos, very strict family. We went through the program together. I, um, I stayed an extra year to get my master's in administration. MaryBeth got a job teaching at Poly. Science. She was kind of a nerd. You know your way around Long Beach, I assume?"

"I live on 2nd."

"You know there are some edgy bars on fourth near Atlantic."

"Yes," I said, though I wasn't well versed in the area's straight bars.

"Every once in a while, MaryBeth liked to pick up a guy. I mean, she was single, and maybe it wasn't—"

"No judgement," I said.

"She picked up Manny Richards one night. He raped her. Beat her up. Hurt her. Badly. I tried to get her to go to the police, but she wouldn't. I mean, she *was* in a bar looking for sex—just not like that. She knew what they'd say about her. And her family. They would never have understood."

"Do you know where Manny Richards is now?"

"Corcoran."

"He's in prison?"

"Yes. About two years after MaryBeth was raped he was arrested for raping another woman, and then two others came forward."

"Did MaryBeth—"

"Right after he was arrested she killed herself. She felt responsible for the other women who were raped."

"That was not her fault," I said.

"No. It wasn't." She took a deep breath. "He's up for parole in three years. I'm planning to go and speak against it, as MaryBeth's friend. It's the least I can do."

Now I knew where Dix was. Was that all I needed? Did I need to ask more questions? After a moment, I said, "I'm sorry about your friend."

"Me too."

Back in the parking lot, I sat in the Jeep not quite ready to start it. I rolled down the window and squinted at the bright afternoon. Everything looked a bit faded, a bit washed out, as though the bright colors were afraid to come out in the sun.

What I was doing was important. It mattered. At first, I thought that was just because Danny Osborne had been unjustly imprisoned. Now I was seeing that a false conviction had ramifications well beyond the person convicted. Women were raped because Manny Richards didn't go to prison for killing Audrey Gunderson. Women died because Manny Richards had remained free. Convicting the wrong person had rippled through a community. Many were harmed, many suffered.

TWENTY

February 20, 1996
Tuesday evening

I went home. As I was walking in, I tried Lydia one more time on the cellular. She didn't answer, so I decided not to leave a message.

In the kitchen, I found Ronnie cooking dinner with Junior looking on. A glass of wine sat in front of Junior.

"What are you making?" I asked. There was a *Martha Stewart Living* magazine open on the counter.

"Polenta lasagna," Ronnie said.

"It's Martha's idea of a romantic meal," Junior added. "Wink, wink."

I flipped the magazine closed for a moment so I could see the cover. Cloth hearts with ribbons and a list of the articles inside.

"We can make lampshades later," I commented.

"Don't be mean," Ronnie said. "Junior was telling me how much fun Long Beach was when the naval base was fully staffed." It was currently being shut down. Or maybe it was shut down. They kept going back and forth.

Junior said, "I've always adored a man in dress whites. In the seventies, all you had to do was whisper the word ensign in my ear and I was hard as steel."

"Thanks for the image," I said.

"How's your case?" Ronnie wanted to know. I was beginning to worry about my dinner. The lasagna was still in little piles all around the kitchen. It didn't seem that it would get into the glass baking dish anytime soon. I went to the refrigerator and got myself a pop.

"It's going well. I can't talk too much about it."

"Attorney-client privilege," Junior said, as though the two of us might not know that.

"Actually, I have information I haven't given to my boss yet. She should really hear it first."

"You're going to get this poor kid out of prison, aren't you?" Ronnie asked. Kid? They were roughly the same age. I almost pointed that out, but then I thought we've all frozen Danny in time. He'll never be more than that teenager convicted of murder.

"Yes. We have to."

"You'll have to tell us all about it when it's over," Junior said.

'Say, I hope I didn't cross any lines when I let Mrs. Chen in last night."

"What?" Ronnie asked. "What are you talking about?"

"Darling, your mother was here. Didn't you...?"

Despite seeing Ronnie before bed and briefly in the morning, I did not tell him about his mother's visit.

"Oh my, I've put my foot in it again haven't I?" I'd begun to think Junior was most comfortable with his foot in it.

"Why was she here?" Ronnie wanted to know. "Did you tell her I don't want her here?"

"Not in so many words."

"What did you talk about?"

"She attempted to sell me on the idea of the two of us having a wife together."

"Actually, that sounds lovely," Junior said. There was an awkward silence which he decided to fill with, "I hope this isn't overstepping, but I have to say the iceberg that sank the Titanic had more warmth than your mother."

Ronnie ignored the comment and asked me, "Were you going to tell me she was here?"

"No, I hadn't planned to." I gave Junior what I hoped was a very dirty look.

"Why not? Why would you lie to me?"

"Oh darling, that's not a lie. He just didn't tell you."

I was too accomplished a liar not to understand a lie of omission, so I didn't try that defense. "I'm not sure you're ready to hear what she had to say."

"She said she wanted me to get married. I've heard that—" but then he stopped. He seemed to realize there was more. "Junior, could you leave us alone for a minute."

"Of course, if there's one thing I've learned it's how to make a graceful exit."

Graceful would have been leaving before he'd been asked to. He scooted over to the fridge and quickly opened it up and poured himself some more wine. Some more of *our* wine. He seemed to read my mind as he said, "I'll buy some wine as soon as my disability check arrives."

Neither Ronnie or I responded as Junior slunk out of the room with his filled-to-the-rim glass of wine. We were quiet. The kitchen was quiet—well, except for the sound of a dog barking two or three houses down. Finally, Ronnie said, "I know you lie about the past. I'm kind of okay with that. I mean, sometimes I think it's better I don't know. But you never lie to me about now. You're always truthful about the things going on with us now. Except for this..."

And except for the fact that I'd lied about being bashed. I felt a pang of guilt—well, several pangs. Actually, I was beginning to feel like a guilt pin cushion. I was going to have to tell the truth. I was also going to have to admit I was wrong not to tell him his mother had been here.

"Basically, your mother said she wouldn't be coming back. That I wouldn't be seeing her again."

"Drama queen," Ronnie said, under his breath.

"Telling you seemed to make it final. I was afraid there might not be any going back if I told you." And as soon as I said it, it sounded awfully paternal. Something I tried not to be. Because of our age difference I tried to avoid making decisions for Ronnie. "I'm sorry, I shouldn't have done that."

He looked a bit confused for a moment and then asked, "Do you really think I'll never see my mother again?"

———

February 21, 1996
Wednesday Morning

I was barely awake when my cursed cellular phone began to ring. It took a few minutes to figure out that it was in my pants and my pants were on the floor. After we finished fighting, Ronnie and I had had make-up sex and our clothes had ended up all over the place. I got out of bed and took the cellular phone out of my pants pocket.

"Hello?" I said, quietly. Ronnie was still sleeping.

"It's Lydia. Can you meet me at the Park Pantry for breakfast?"

"Sure. When?"

"Now?"

"Oh. Okay."

"Is everything okay?"

"No. It's not."

Park Pantry was on the corner of Junipero and Broadway. It was an upscale diner which happened to be my favorite breakfast spot in town. There was a counter, where I often sat, and booths along both the Broadway and Junipero sides. There was a small lobby as you walked in where you had to wait for the hostess/manager to seat you.

On the weekends, people would be spilling out into the street. It was a Wednesday though, so I was alone in the lobby. I saw Lydia sitting in a booth on the Broadway side. I waved at my favorite waitress, a tall, square-faced woman named Cindy, and walked over to join Lydia.

"I have a lot of news," I said.

"Hold onto it for a minute. Something's happened."

I was about to ask what exactly, but Cindy was there setting a coffee cup down in front of me. She filled it from the pot she had in her other hand and then refilled Lydia's coffee.

"You want your regular?" she asked me.

"Yes, please. And an orange muffin."

"You got it." Then she asked Lydia, "Did you decide what you'd like honey?"

"I'll have what he's having," she said, though I was sure she didn't know what that was.

Cindy said, "Okie doke," and walked off.

"It's an ABC omelet," I explained. Avocado, bacon and cheese.

She nodded.

"With wheat toast."

She nodded again. On the seat next to her was a giant leather tote. From it she took out a micro-recorder in a plastic bag. She set it down on the table between us. Through the bag she pressed the play button. I was expecting a recording of a threat, probably one delivered on the telephone. Instead, I listened as Lydia attempted to purchase crystal.

Which made no sense at all. Crystal. Tina. Ice. All names for meth, a popular drug in the gay community. I was used to seeing tweakers with their jerky movements and their chemical smell. I'd never noticed any of that with Lydia.

"Explain this," I said.

"Just listen," she said, starting the tape over.

I listened. 'I want ice,' she said on the tape. 'And I want a fair price.'

'Ice isn't cheap,' a man said, sounding like a drug dealer from Central Casting.

'But that's what I want.'

'How much do you want?'

'Three, four.'

'Grams?'

'Of course.'

'Here, put it in your purse. Don't let anyone see you.'

The tape ended. Lydia said, "It was sent to my husband."

"How do you think they made it?"

"I met with a painter on Monday. He had a color chip and kept talking about this color called Winter Ice. Really it was a dreadful color. It looked mint green to me. I kept saying no, but he kept coming back to it. Finally, I said, 'I don't want Winter Ice.' They sliced that up until I said, 'I want ice.'"

"They did a good job," I said.

"We were inside. They added street sounds. That makes it sound like we're outside. I think that helps cover up the splices."

"There aren't that many splices to begin with, are there?"

"No. There's 'I want ice' and 'three, four.' I'd actually said, 'I'd like you to be finished in three, four days.'"

"Did Dwayne believe this?"

She shrugged. "Probably not."

Taking a deep breath, she followed it with a sigh. "After law school, I had a job with a very prestigious firm. Everyone there was doing coke. I had a problem for a while. It's one of the reasons I don't practice that kind of law."

"Were you ever arrested?"

"No, no. Thankfully. One of my coworkers was. He nearly lost his license. But then the firm found a loophole and everything was dropped."

"Do you think your name might have come up in the investigation?"

"Why do you ask that?"

"Because the person behind the tape knows your history."

"I thought they just got lucky. I mean, I never did meth. Oh God, you're probably right."

"It's Montero."

"Why do you say that?"

"Because Aaron Angler was Montero's stepson. I found out yesterday when I met with Deborah Daly. They were married for nearly ten years. Montero knew Aaron Angler and Manny Richards killed Audrey Gunderson right from the start. He knew when he was getting Danny to confess."

"Wait. Who's Manny Richards?"

"Dix. He's a convicted rapist serving time in Corcoran."

"He's in the same prison as Danny?"

Our breakfasts arrived. Cindy set them in front of us. I was starving and wanted to dive right in, but I felt like I should wait for Lydia. This was a lot to absorb so I gave her a moment.

"Do you want me to talk to Dwayne?"

"What would that do?"

"I'm a bartender. Some of my customers are meth heads. I know what it looks like."

"No. It's fine. He's making me take a drug test. It's the only thing he'll believe."

TWENTY-ONE

February 21, 1996
Wednesday afternoon

The rest of the day was surprisingly anticlimactic. When we got to the office, Lydia asked Karen and me to pull together everything we had into one file. That meant I had to put together notes on the witnesses I'd spoken to. Karen and Lydia had the only computers in the office—not that I knew much about them—so when Karen took lunch, she set me up at her desk and had me type in my notes.

"Do you know Office 95?"

"Um, no..."

"Great."

She opened a document and said, "Put everything in here. I'll separate them later. This is how you save." She showed me how to navigate the menu to save the file.

"Do that a lot."

"Okay."

I'm not a bad typist, though I'm of the two-fingered variety and it had been a long time since I'd hunted and pecked my way around a keyboard. I was part way through the notes for my second interview, when Lydia came out of her office and said, "Let's look at the DNA test again. Someone changed that report. We need to know who. And we need to know why."

"There was a name on the report. Should I go down and talk to her?" I asked. "I still have some interviews to type up, though."

"Let's think about this. The woman who signed the report, Susan—no, Sylvia. She's probably not the person who altered the report. Her name is on it. She'd also have the least to gain, wouldn't she?"

"Maybe. But maybe she's connected somehow, maybe someone is blackmailing her."

"True. But she would have been assigned randomly, which means it's unlikely she'd be connected. It also makes it difficult to blackmail her—since she probably got the sample the day she wrote the report. There'd be no time to set that up."

"So, it has to be someone more important?"

Lydia nodded.

"Both initials are basically unreadable," I pointed out.

She thought for a moment and said, "Let me make a call." She went back to her office and I went back to work typing into Office 95—and saving. I remembered to save.

I was almost through my notes on the trip to Happy Acres when Karen came back from lunch. "Are you almost done?"

"I need another twenty minutes probably."

"Okay. I'll go in the back and read a few letters."

She hung her parka on the back of the chair I was sitting in and disappeared. I went back to typing. I was nearly finished when Lydia came back out.

"Okay," she started.

"Hold on one sec," I said, finishing up. "Okay. I'm all ears."

"I talked to Sylvia Pope. She said the initials belong to Karen Littlefield and Eric Ralston. Littlefield is a peer; Ralston is a supervisor."

"Then it's Ralston. If it was Littlefield, she'd have to pass it on with the alteration. And she probably wouldn't want to. Ralston might notice. And if he did, she'd be on the hot seat. Did you ask Sylvia Pope about the change?"

"No. I just said I couldn't read the initials. I made it sound almost clerical."

"What made you pick Double Helix?" I asked.

"They're accredited. And they didn't have a backlog."

"Do you think it's possible they might want the county's business."

"I don't have any reason to think that. And I have no reason not to."

"Do you think Eric Ralston would have anything to do with the contact?"

"That's what we have to find out," she said.

Fifteen minutes later, Karen came back and I got out of her way. She applied her computer skills to searching the three names we had at Double Helix in addition to looking into Double Helix itself. I spent nearly an hour arranging what we had for Danny's file.

At just after five, we met in Lydia's office. Karen began, "So, the three people at Double Helix, I'm not seeing anything unusual money-wise. They live in neighborhoods that you'd expect. They drive appropriate vehicles. Ralston has the most expenses, but he probably makes the most money. Sylvia Pope has a daughter at USC, but I found an article about Jewel Pope receiving a scholarship. Her father died about eight years ago, so she'd be getting social security *and* financial aid. There is a recent second mortgage on Pope's house, so I think that tuition is accounted for. I looked around for stories on Double Helix. They're getting work but no contracts with the county or the district attorney."

"Anything about the county farming out work?" Lydia asked.

"Nothing that I could find."

"Hold on a minute. May I?" I asked, pointing at Lydia's phone. She nodded. I asked Karen, "What's the number for the district attorney's office?"

She read it off to me. Both of the women were carefully watching me. When the call was answered, I told the receptionist I worked for a company called DNA-R-US and wanted to speak to the person who handled their forensic work. When I said DNA-R-US both Lydia and Karen rolled their eyes, but the receptionist put me through to a Farley Smith. I began my spiel: "I work for DNA-R-US and we'd like to come in and discuss what we might be able to do for the Orange County District—"

"Hold it right there," Farley said. "You're too late. We closed bidding a month ago."

"Oh, I see. Well, that's unfortunate."

I asked if he could tell me who got the contract, but he said that a decision was still pending. I thanked him and hung up.

"They've just closed bidding on a contract for their DNA work."

Lydia frowned. "If someone from the District Attorney's Office put pressure on them to change a DNA report, that would be major corruption."

"And you don't think that's possible?" Karen asked.

"Of course, it's possible. It's just, why Danny? Why is it so important to keep him in jail? And if you're going to change the report, why not just say the DNA matched?"

"Because you could have that verified," I suggested. "And for all they know you're doing that now."

"It looks like a typo," Karen said. "It's that thing Reagan invented: plausible deniability. If you figure it out, they can say they made a mistake."

"Meanwhile, they're hoping there's one guy, not two."

"Which one of the boys don't they want us to find?" Lydia asked.

"Manny Richards," Karen and I answered at once.

———

I deliberately hung around until Karen went home that night. When she was gone, I leaned into Lydia's office and asked, "So, are you okay?"

"Of course, I'm okay," she bristled.

"The fake painter, what did he look like?"

She shrugged. "Not much taller than me. Kind of wide."

"Muscular, stocky."

"Yeah."

"Short hair."

She nodded. "One of the guys who beat you up, right?"

"Sounds like cops."

She cringed.

"Probably buddies of Montero's."

"Why though?" She wondered.

"Really? He put an innocent kid in prison to protect his own stepson. That's gotta have consequences."

"We don't do consequences, though. We're just trying to get Danny out of prison."

"It'll cross the district attorney's desk at some point, won't it?"

"They won't want to do anything. It'll put every single case he worked on in question. That's a nightmare they'll want to avoid."

"So, nothing will happen to him?" I asked, almost stunned.

"I doubt it," Lydia said.

"Then why? Why is he trying to stop us?" I asked, borrowing her question. "Pride? He doesn't want anyone to know he was a bad cop?"

"Dom, sometimes you can't figure these people out. They think differently."

"He should be in prison."

"I know. But that's not our job."

"Justice isn't our job?"

"Only for Danny."

———

I left a few minutes later, but I didn't go home. Instead, I drove down to Happy Acres. I sat in front of Peggy McCallister's trailer for a few minutes. It was dark and the red Civic was gone. I didn't have the patience to wait around until she came home. I had a hunch where she might be, so I decided to check it out.

John Barleycorn's Tap Room sat at the end of the mini-mall next to the check-cashing place. Its glass windows had been painted black inside and its name was in gold. I parked in front; there were only a handful of cars—one of which was Peggy McCallister's Civic.

Inside the smoky bar, I could see that the walls were cranberry, the stools and booths brown. The bar itself was on one side and was well-stocked. Behind the bar was a pretty barmaid with bright red hair. I sat down and ordered a Miller Lite. I didn't enjoy light beers and was unlikely to finish it. I only ordered it to be polite.

Of course, I'd seen Peggy as soon as I walked in. She was sitting in one of the booths with her back to me. Sitting across from her was one of the guys who beat me up. Bingo.

When the barmaid set my beer down in front of me, I put down a twenty and asked, "Do you know the name of that guy with Peggy McCallister?"

She looked at me suspiciously. I was a stranger and yet I knew the name of one of her customers—by my guess, one of her regular customers.

"You can keep the change by the way."

After a moment, she picked up the twenty and said, "Ernie Sanchez. He's a cop."

"Yeah, I figured." Then something occurred to me. "He have a friend named Garcia?"

"You have another twenty?" I did, so she continued, "Renaldo Garcia. Also, a cop."

"Thanks."

The barmaid walked away, and I sipped the watery beer while watching Sanchez and Peggy. Every so often she'd throw her head back and laugh. I was pretty sure she was laughing at her own jokes since his mouth didn't do much in the way of moving. With only a half-formed idea in my head, I got off the stool and walked over.

I looked right at Sanchez, and said, "You probably shouldn't have spit on me."

"I don't know what you're talking about," he said, not looking at me.

"Yeah. You do," I said. I glanced back at Peggy, she looked like she might be ready to puke. "Here's the deal, Sanchez. You can go down for what you did to me, assault and battery, or you can give us Montero."

He looked me hard in the eye, and said, "You don't have anything."

"Like I said, you shouldn't have spit on me."

And then I walked out of the bar. I drove directly home. The night I was attacked, I'd stripped my shirt off at some point and thrown it into the hamper in the corner of our bedroom. I hadn't done the laundry. Neither had Ronnie.

We weren't the neatest people in the world. We managed to keep the kitchen relatively clean and that was about the best we could do. The rest of our house would have gone to hell in a hand basket if Ronnie hadn't hired a company called Happy Home to clean the place twice a month.

Originally, they weren't doing our laundry, but after Ronnie had to go buy extra underwear to go to work we added that service. They came on Thursdays. I was pretty sure they were due the following day.

When I got home, I ran upstairs to our bedroom. I was horrified to find that the hamper was not there and the bed had been stripped. What was going on? Why on earth would Ronnie do the laundry the day before we were paying someone—

I ran downstairs and then down to our tiny basement where the washer and dryer were. There was Junior, loading the washing machine.

"What the fuck are you doing?"

"Laundry," he said, a confused look on his face.

"*Our* laundry? Really?"

"Well, I needed a few things. Barely enough for a load, so I thought—"

I pushed him aside and dug through the remaining clothes and found the shirt I'd worn Friday night to work. "Oh, thank God."

"That's the shirt you got beat up in," Junior said. "You know, I have a trick for getting out bloodstains."

"Don't go into our bedroom," I said, flatly.

"I was just trying to—"

"Don't. Just don't."

TWENTY-TWO

February 22, 1996
Thursday morning

I was late for work the next morning. Around seven, I'd gone down to the Long Beach Police Department and filled out an incident report on my beating. I gave them my bloodied shirt—complete with spittle—walked them through a long explanation on how I knew the names of my assailants, gave them the names of my friends who'd seen me hours after it happened: Ronnie, John and Junior, and let them take photographs of the week-old bruises all over my torso.

Maybe I'm wrong, but it seemed like the bruising was sticking around a lot longer than it had from my younger scrapes. Many of the bruises were still in the brown range and wouldn't see yellow for days. It must be part of getting older. Bad things hang around longer than they used to.

Anyway, I walked into the Freedom Agenda around ten. Karen looked up at me and yelled, "He's here!"

Lydia rushed out of her office, pulling her jacket on, and carrying a briefcase. "You're late."

"I had something important to do."

"Right now, Danny Osborne is the only important thing you're doing. We have to hurry," she said, opening the front door. I followed. She turned and said, "Bring that," pointing at two banker's boxes bungy-ed to a wheeled cart.

I grabbed it and followed her out to her BMW. She opened the trunk and I picked up the boxes and cart—my ribs squealed a bit, but I ignored them. I laid the whole thing in the back. Lydia slammed the lid shut and we were off.

"Our meeting is at eleven," she explained as she sped down the city street. "Vance Piper will be there. I told him to bring Montero."

"Aren't we going in the wrong direction?" I asked. We were driving up Atlantic toward the 405. To go to Orange County, we'd have turned on 7th and picked up the freeway—

"We have a conference room booked at Edwin's firm, Karpinski & Karpinski. Their offices are on Figueroa. Downtown L.A."

I had several questions about that. "Karpinski & Karpinski? Father and son?"

"Brothers. Edwin's younger, making him the second Karpinski."

"And... how did you get Piper to agree to this? I mean, he's the chief ADA of Orange County. Why would he drive up to L.A.? Why wouldn't he insist we come to him?"

Lydia concentrated on driving, zigging in and out of traffic. Then, "I don't know. I was expecting a protracted negotiation about where we'd meet, downtown L.A. was my opening salvo, and then he just said yes."

"Maybe he's got an afternoon appointment," I suggested.

"He could be heading up to Big Bear afterward. Taking a three-day weekend," she said.

Neither of us believed either of those things. Something was off about this. We just didn't know what. As we got onto the 405 going north, she asked, "So, what was so important this morning?"

"I filed an incident report on my attack."

"I thought you weren't planning on doing that?"

"Ernie Sanchez and Renaldo Garcia," I said simply.

"And who are they?"

"The guys who beat me up. They're probably narcs. They had something to do with Duncan Osborne. I found Ernie Sanchez with Peggy McCallister in a bar last night."

"You didn't speak to him, did you?"

"Briefly."

"Briefly. What did you say?" I could tell this wasn't going well, and that she probably wasn't going to like what I'd said.

"I told him he shouldn't have spit on me. And that he needs to be ready to give up Montero."

"I should have known," she said under her breath.

"What do you mean by that?" I asked.

She ignored me though, and said, "Dom, you shouldn't have done that."

"Why not?" I asked, though I knew what she was going to say. It wasn't our job to find Audrey's killer. It was just our job to—

"You may have screwed everything up. For one thing, the crime you're trying to leverage took place in Long Beach, Los Angeles County. Montero's crimes are in Orange County. You have a jurisdictional problem."

"That can't be worked out?"

"I'm not done. Cops don't like to go after cops. District attorneys don't like to go after cops. You're basically asking the Long Beach police and city prosecutor to go after not just the two cops who beat you up but a third cop not in their jurisdiction—for which they'll need the cooperation of the Orange County District Attorney's Office and possibly the Westmoreland Police Department. You're attempting to create a kind of Rube Goldberg prosecution. If any of the pieces doesn't work, the whole thing doesn't work."

She was right, of course. There were a lot of moving parts and I didn't control any of them. The problem was, I'd already set it in motion. *And*, it was the only way I could see to get justice for Amy.

"You think I've screwed things up for Danny?"

"We need Vance Piper to give up. If he joined our petition, Danny would be out in days. Dropping a political hot potato into his lap isn't going to help things. I'm not sure I can bring you into the meeting now."

"O-kay," I said, not really understanding.

"If I bring you into the meeting and introduce you, it will be like I'm threatening them. You've turned yourself into a weapon. I like to try good old logic before I start threatening people."

Which made her a different kind of attorney in my book.

———

The offices of Karpinski & Karpinski were located in a gray building that bore a striking resemblance to a cheese grater. Lydia drove down a long ramp into the underground parking and then relinquished the Beemer to a valet.

"Make sure I get that validated," she said to me, as she put the ticket into her purse. Then we walked over to the elevator that took us up to the lobby.

We stopped at the security desk and signed in. Then, I followed her up to the 32nd floor. There were several other businesses on the floor. We walked down a long hallway to a set of shiny walnut double doors that said KARPINSKI & KARPINKSI in Art Deco-inspired brass. Lydia threw one of the doors open, and we were in a nicely appointed waiting room, butter-colored walls and burgundy leather chairs. A pretty girl sat behind a mahogany desk. On the desk were a large telephone with a lot of buttons and a computer that hadn't been turned on.

"I'm Lydia Gonsalez. We're the first ones here, right?"

"Um, I guess," the girl said. "No one's really said anything to me."

"What's your name?"

"Miranda."

"Miranda, this is my investigator, Dom Reilly. He's going to be waiting out here with you." Then to me, "The brothers stack all their meetings, so they only have to have a receptionist one day a week." Back to Miranda, "Can you boot up the computer?"

"I can but I'm really more of a Mac person."

"That's okay," Lydia said. "You're an actress, right?"

The girl brightened. "I *am*."

"When people come in, act like you work here all the time. Act like you're busy. Can you do that?"

"Absolutely." She quickly glanced at the things on her desk which had suddenly become props.

"Great," Lydia said. "We're going down to the conference room."

I followed her through another door and down a hallway. Six closed doors, four on the outside wall and two on the inside. Lydia opened one of the inside doors, revealing a windowless conference room. I took the boxes off the rack and put them on the table. I doubted anyone would read anything in them. They were part of the performance, though.

Perhaps Miranda wasn't the only actress.

"How did you know she was an actress?" I asked.

"There's a temp agency that does the industry. They're a go-to for the brothers. She's probably devastated she's not working at Paramount today."

"You just want me to sit in the lobby with her?"

"Yes. Try and look like you're waiting for one of the brothers."

I wasn't entirely sure how to do that, but nodded anyway. I was sorry I was going to miss the meeting. I would have liked to have seen the look on their faces when Lydia laid everything out. Actually, I would have liked to see their faces; I wasn't even sure what they looked like.

"What if it doesn't go well?"

"I guess we'll be going to court then."

"That's not what I mean."

She looked at me blankly a moment then said, "Nothing's going to happen. Yes, Montero got you beat-up and he's probably behind that ridiculous recording, but he's hardly going to attack me in front of the chief ADA."

I wasn't quite as convinced, but she was the boss.

"I'll be in the lobby then."

I walked back down the long hallway and into the waiting room. I grabbed a magazine, *Time*. The cover story was "The Golden Geeks," which was all about the World Wide Web and the people who were making money off it. The guy on the cover had something to do with Netscape. I'd heard of Netscape, but I didn't know much about it. I could barely handle AOL and everyone said that was incredibly easy.

Continuing through the magazine, I found articles on the election, which was still more than half a year away, violence on TV and the "V" chip—which was as alien to me as Netscape, and a fight Joan Collins was having with her publisher. I was deep into the story about how her publisher was shocked, absolutely shocked, when Collins delivered a manuscript they found unpublishable, when a man walked into the waiting room.

He was not especially tall, was bald on top with white tufts on the side, and a little mustache. He could have been Cesar Romero's less attractive brother. He told Miranda, "I have a meeting with Vance Piper and Lydia Gonsalez."

"And you are?"

"Samuel Montero."

"Of course," Miranda said. "Why don't you have a seat, Mr. Montero. They should be ready for you momentarily."

"Thank you," he replied and then sat down across from me. He picked up *People* magazine, which was running *The Honeymooners* on their cover for some kind of nostalgia edition. He opened the magazine while I stared at a picture of Gene Kelly up in the corner. He'd died recently, but apparently still needed the publicity.

Subtly, I looked Montero up and down. He was a complete disappointment. He didn't look evil or slimy or even remotely dangerous. He looked like someone's grandfather. He should be bouncing little children on his knee and complaining about how much it cost to feed his dog. He shouldn't be here answering questions about how he'd sent an innocent teenager to prison to protect his own stepson, his own guilty stepson.

I was wondering if I could strike up a conversation with him just to see what he'd say, when the door opened and in walked Vance Piper. He was tall and slender with blond hair that flopped over his forehead like a kid's. He was probably in his early forties, but you could only tell it when he smiled. His whole face crinkled.

And he was smiling. A lot.

"Sammy! It's so good to see you. It's been a long time. How's Sylvie?"

"She's good."

"And the cancer?"

"In remission."

They knew each other. Well, obviously. A moment later, Vance lowered his voice and said, "Don't worry about this. She doesn't have anything real. Say as little as possible. We're just going to stonewall her."

"I got a call this morning—" Montero started.

Miranda interrupted. "You're Mr. Piper, aren't you?"

"I am."

"I think Ms. Gonsalez is ready for you. If you'd like to follow me." I had no idea if Miranda knew where the conference room was, though obviously she was game for the hunt.

They know each other. Suddenly that seemed like the most important thing in the world. How well did they know each other? And then something Deborah Daly had said popped into my head: Piglet and Dix had been friends a very long time. But Larry Tribble had said that Dix transferred to their school for the final year. That meant they didn't meet at school, they'd met earlier somewhere else.

Miranda wasn't back yet. I went over to the reception desk and picked up the phone. I tried calling the office. I had trouble. Did I need to put in the area code? Did I need to dial a number for an outside—

Screw it. I got out my cellular phone and punched in the number for the Freedom Agenda. Karen answered.

"I need Deborah Daly's phone number."

"Hello to you too."

"Sorry, it's important."

I sat down again, sunk into the leather chair, and waited. She was back, "310-433—"

"Hold on," I said, getting up and going back to the desk. I grabbed a pen and a Post-It pad. "Go ahead." She gave me the number and I wrote it down.

"What's going on?" she wanted to know.

"The meeting's just starting. There's something I need to find out for Lydia. I'll tell you later."

And then I clicked off. I carefully pressed the number into the phone —really the buttons were almost too small for my fingers—then waited while it rang. The call was picked up.

"Mrs. Daly?"

"Yes."

"This is Dom Reilly. Do you have a moment? I have a quick question. It's important."

"All right."

"You said that Aaron and Manny knew each other for a long time. But I've been told that Manny wasn't at Westmoreland High until his senior year."

"That's right. My husband and I were friends with Manny's mother, Meg Richards."

"Your husband, Samuel Montero."

"Yes. I meant my second husband."

That wasn't the connection I was looking for. "And, who was Manny's father?"

"Meg was kind of wild. She'd married and divorced very young but not to Manny's father. We didn't talk much about that."

These weren't the answers I was looking for. There had to be a connection to Piper. I realized I might be asking this the wrong way, "Now, how do you know Vance Piper?"

"Well, Vance is Meg's brother," she said, sounding a little confused that I didn't know this.

"Vance Piper is Manny's uncle?"

"Yes. He took a special interest because Manny's father wasn't in the picture. We were *all* friends. We did a lot together. Potlucks, holidays—"

"Thank you. You've been a big help."

I clicked off. Holy shit. Lydia was in there with the two men responsible for putting our client in prison and she didn't have all the information she needed. She'd told me a couple times that a lawyer should never ask a question without knowing the answer to it. But she was in there missing one big answer—

I grabbed the Post-It pad again and wrote, "VP is Manny's Uncle." Then I hurried down the hall. Miranda was opening doors. She looked at me with a panic-stricken face.

"I offered them coffee, but now I can't find the break room."

I shrugged. I had no idea which door it was behind, or even if there was one. I reached the conference room. Tapped on the door and walked in. The packets we'd prepared were sitting in front of them unopened. Good, they hadn't really started. I sat down next to Lydia. She gave me a questioning look as I handed her the Post-It. She read it, folded it and sat quietly for a moment. I could tell she was reworking her strategy.

"What's happening?" Piper asked.

"This is Dom Reilly, my investigator," she replied. Then directly to Montero, she said, "Your friends Ernie Sanchez and Renaldo Garcia beat him up last week. But then you know that."

"That's an appalling accusation, Ms. Gonsalez," Piper said.

"What's appalling is that it's true," she said, not giving him time to respond, she continued. "Your nephew is Emmanuel Richards."

"Yes, Manny is my nephew. That has nothing to do with this."

"Except that he and Aaron Angler raped and murdered Amy Gunderson," I said, inserting myself.

"You have absolutely no proof of that."

"We have DNA evidence, as you know," Lydia said. "And, your

nephew is a convicted rapist currently in prison. It shouldn't be difficult to collect his DNA. We know where he is."

I watched Piper's face carefully. He was weighing his options. There weren't many. We'd obviously identified Manny as a suspect. There wasn't a reasonable way for Piper to stand in the way of his DNA being collected.

"You're making a mistake," Montero said. "You'll regret—"

"Shut up, Sam," Piper said. He licked his lips, his decision made. "It snowballed. The whole thing. It just—the boys had gotten into some trouble. Drugs mostly."

"Don't do this, Van," Montero said. "You can't—"

"We pulled strings, Sam and me. When the Gunderson thing happened, by that time he had me over a barrel. If I didn't go along, I'd be exposed for giving breaks to my nephew. I'd have been finished."

"So you put a teenager in prison," Lydia said.

"He was a drug addict," Montero said.

"And your stepson was a rapist," I said.

"He was a good boy," Montero said. "I loved his mother. I loved him. I shouldn't have let him hang around with Manny. That's where I went wrong."

Piper looked like he might defend his nephew but then thought better of it. Manny's crimes were proven. They were indefensible. Finally, he said, "Go ahead and file your petition. We'll join it based on the DNA evidence."

"You can't do that, Van. You have to fight—"

"You want something in return," Lydia said, "don't you?"

It took a moment before Piper said anything. The silence was cracking, alive. He inhaled deeply, and said, "I've been with the DA's office for almost twenty years. If this comes out all my cases will be suspect. All those convictions will be in jeopardy. Real criminals, violent criminals. They could be released from prison. People will get hurt, people will die."

"I'm here to get Danny Osborne out of prison," Lydia said. "That's my only job."

Piper nodded then said, "Then this is over."

"Wait a minute," Montero said. We all turned to look at him. He pointed at me. "We need this one to get down to the Long Beach Police and recant his incident report."

Basically, he wanted me to 'drop' the charges, but as a former police officer he knew I couldn't exactly do that. He also knew all I had to do to make the charges go away was to stop cooperating. Or at least, that's what he thought. The DNA samples I provided made it possible my testimony wouldn't be required.

"I didn't have anything to do with that," Piper said. "That was all Sam." Then he looked at his friend, and said, "You're on your own."

"Uh-uh. I go down, you go down."

The two men stared at each other. For just a second, I thought they might jump across the table and beat the crap out of each other. But then Lydia said, "He'll do it. He'll recant."

Anger washed through me. What was she doing? Had I missed something? Did she want these guys to get away with this? Whose side was she on?

"I think we're done," she said, standing up. Reluctantly, Montero got up. He and Piper stalked out of the room.

"What the fuck was that?" I asked.

"Calm down. This is far from over."

"I don't get it."

"I'll file my motion. Piper will join the motion by the end of the day. Danny should be out of prison next week."

"That's great, but it doesn't answer my question."

"As soon as Danny's out we'll find him a civil attorney. All the information we have will go to that attorney. I'm bound to do that legally. The first thing Danny's new attorney will do is threaten to release what we've learned about Piper and Montero. The DA in Orange County will want to shut that down, so they'll put a nice juicy settlement onto the table. Piper will quietly lose his job; Montero will likely lose his pension."

"They belong in prison," I said.

"I don't disagree with you. But we have to be realistic. They deserve to be punished. And they will be."

"Do I really have to recant my statement?"

"Up to you. They're very unlikely to do anything about it, anyway. You know that."

And I did.

TWENTY-THREE

February 22, 1996
Late Thursday morning

The first thing we did when we got back to the office was fill Karen in on what had happened. Then it was lunchtime and Lydia decided we all needed to go home early. I'd already told Lydia I wasn't coming in on Friday—I was really too old for a fifteen-hour day. She didn't mind at all.

When I pulled up in front of our house, I saw Ronnie sitting on the front stoop next to four small boxes.

"Hey, you're home early."

"Our guy should be out of prison next week."

"That's great."

"What are the boxes?"

"My baby clothes, toys, kindergarten report card, photo albums…"

"Your mother dropped them off?"

He nodded. "I'm thinking of throwing them away."

"Don't do that."

"Why not? I'm just going to put them in the attic and never look at them again."

"Your mother will want them back some day."

"No, she won't."

"People can change."

"Have you *met* my mother?"

"You're her only son. You're really all that matters to her. She's playing chicken. All you have to do is hold on until she realizes she can't win."

I wasn't sure that was entirely true. Some people held onto anger their entire lives. I didn't have any reason to think that Mai was any different than that.

"It doesn't matter," he said. "I have you. You're my family."

And that made me feel guilty. I'd lied to him about being bashed. I'd lied to him about a hundred things. But maybe that's what family was, people you lied to for their own good.

"Yes, I'm your family."

———

February 25, 1996
Sunday Evening

Life went back to what it had been before the dinner at La Bohéme, before I'd met Lydia Gonsalez, before I'd met Danny Osborne. I went to work at the Hawk, talked to my regulars about politics—half of them wanted to vote for Bob Dole because they thought he'd make them rich like Reagan had, except Reagan hadn't made them rich he'd just made them think they could be, TV—they all wanted to screw George Clooney, and believed Michael Jackson's marriage to Lisa Marie Presley was every bit the sham it looked like. Typical.

I didn't say anything about getting an innocent guy out of prison or failing to punish the people who'd put him there. In my slower moments, I wondered what it would be like for Audrey's family to find out the boy they'd hated, the boy they'd happily seen punished, was not the person who'd killed her. What would that do to them?

I tried to spend extra time with Ronnie, but it was pretty hard to do. He was busy with clients, and when he wasn't, I was at the bar. Sunday evening, after beer bust ended, he showed up at the end of my bar. I poured him a Ketel and cran, and brought it down to him.

He didn't say hello.

"The police came by the house."

"Oh yeah? What did they want?"

"They wanted to talk about the night you got beat up. You reported it even though you said you weren't going to."

"I did, yes. I didn't expect them to do anything about it."

"I said something about it being a bashing, that it was because you're gay, but they seemed to think it had something to do with the work you were doing for Lydia. Is that true?"

They'd given him a lot of information they shouldn't have. But then, Ronnie was charming. He could talk to anyone. Or maybe they were just fucking with me.

I said, "It did. Yes."

"Why didn't you tell me?"

"Because you wouldn't want me working for Lydia. And I like it. It matters to me."

"Don't I matter to you?"

"More than anything."

"Then you should have told me."

And I realized something important. When I lied to Ronnie it was always to protect him, to keep him safe from all the things in my past that might reach out and hurt him. But this lie was for me. This was a selfish lie I shouldn't have told.

"You're right. It won't happen again."

He frowned at me. "Why are you giving in so easily?"

"Because you're right."

"Yeah, but you should try harder. It makes for a more satisfying win. Why did you decide to file a report? I mean, you wouldn't have had to tell me if you hadn't."

Then I explained what I'd been trying to do, how I'd saved the spittle covered shirt from the laundry, how I was really going after Montero. I had to stop in the middle and pour him another drink. When I was finished, he asked, "Do you think Lydia's wrong? Do you think they'll actually do something?"

I shrugged. "Maybe. They showed up, didn't they? What did they ask you?"

"What you looked like. If you had emotional problems. If you ever did anything like hurting yourself."

Anger flared. "They think I did that to myself?"

"I don't think so. I think they had to ask the questions."

"Did they talk to John and Junior."

"Junior talked to them forever, and I do mean *forever*."

"Great."

As I served him another drink, he said, "Thank you for telling me. I like knowing things about you."

"You're drunk."

"That's impossible. You barely put any vodka in these things at all."

He'd already had at least five shots.

———

Leap Year 1996
Thursday Afternoon

Danny didn't get out of prison until Thursday afternoon later that week. That morning, we met at The Freedom Agenda and drove up to Corcoran in Lydia's car. We didn't stop for coffee or muffins, and Lydia drove like we were competing in the Indy 500. Once we were out of Los Angeles County, I asked, "How are things with Dwayne? Did you convince him you're not a drug addict?"

"I did. I took a drug test like he asked."

"Oh. That sucks."

"It did. I tried to be mad about it, but if I were in his shoes, I don't know that I'd trust me either."

I suppose that was the best attitude, but I still thought her husband was something of a dick.

I told her the police had been around investigating my assault, but that only resulted in a "hhhmff." She didn't believe they would do much. For that matter, neither did I.

"What happens to Danny?" I asked.

"What do you mean? He gets out of prison today."

"And then? He doesn't seem to have any family or friends."

"Edwin is putting him at the Bonaventure for a week."

"That's not very permanent."

"We're going to need to ask Danny what he wants. It is up to him, after all."

"True."

The prison was not especially welcoming. There were vans from the local stations already in the parking lot when we drove in. None of us were allowed into the prison. There was a lot of milling around as we waited.

I finally met Edwin Karpinski. He was blond and blue-eyed, lithe and thin, obviously athletic. The kind of guy who'd had life handed to him. He certainly wasn't someone who'd ever had to try very hard. He didn't spend much time with Lydia and me, he was too busy talking to the reporters for the L.A. stations, getting ready for the interviews with Danny.

"He's going to take all the credit," I said to Lydia.

"Yes. That's what he's here for."

"You're okay with that?"

"I'm a lawyer, not a TV celebrity."

"Isn't he a lawyer?"

"Not a very good one."

"Ouch."

"He has no idea what he's gotten himself into. When I got Jimmy Claxton out of prison, I received death threats for nearly a month. People don't like to think the system can make mistakes, so they assume I got him out on some evil technicality. Then there are the people from your past who think they can show up and ask you for money. Essentially blackmail, but who likes to use words like that."

Then, they drove Danny out in a van and dropped him in the middle of the circus. News reporters waved microphones in his face. Edwin and an older man I later learned was a civil attorney attempted to move Danny into a position where they could answer questions for him. Danny saw Lydia and me and waved, but we were too far away, and too camera shy to help him.

I tried not to be photographed or videoed. I was acutely aware of all the cameras around me and I wanted to avoid them all. I even jostled one of the TV guys so he'd stop panning in my direction.

The questions being asked were pathetic: "How did it feel to be released from prison?" The question seemed to confuse Danny. So much so, the only answer he could think of was, "I just want a cold beer." The reporters laughed at this but then went back to dumb questions: "Are you angry at the people who put you behind bars?"

"I guess. I mean, it wasn't nice."

"Who do you hold most responsible?"

"I don't know."

Edwin stepped in, "We hold the district attorney of Orange County and the Westmoreland Police Department responsible and will be filing suit shortly."

Fear flickered across Danny's face. I doubted anyone had spoken to him about that beforehand. Clearly, Danny would want some form of compensation, so the fear must have come from the realization that he might be going back to court, that his life would continue to be filled with lawyers and confrontation.

He leaned over and said something quietly to Edwin, but it was the other man who gently took Danny aside and spoke to him until he was nodding his head.

Meanwhile, Edwin fielded questions.

"Can you give us any specifics on how this all occurred?"

"There are always systemic problems when this type of injustice happens. Even when you identify specific bad actors, it's the system that allowed them to flourish."

"Will there be any specific officers named in your suit?"

"I can't answer that at this time."

TWENTY-FOUR

Leap Year 1996
Thursday evening

Who are we? That's a question that follows most of us our entire lives. And the answer is constantly shifting, changing, coming into focus, and then sliding away again. The person you are is not the person you were ten years ago, or even five. It may seem like we're not changing, but we are. The movement happens slowly, or quickly, but it happens. It's always happening.

Something I read once, I don't remember where, but... there isn't such a thing as zero gravity. It's something astronauts experience because the capsule they're in is in a constant state of falling. A capsule doesn't orbit the earth, it falls around it. Gravity hugs them to the planet, and inside the astronauts float. Like a skydiver who never has to land.

That seems to be what we're all doing. Falling through time. And as we fall, we shift, we change, we grow, we become. And we leave so much behind.

It was barely dark when Lydia and I got back to Long Beach. As she got off the freeway, she said, "You did very well. Is it good to get back in the saddle?"

"It was a new experience," I lied. "A good one, mostly."

Ignoring my semi-evasion, she said, "You're going to stick with us, aren't you?"

Something about the way she said that made me wary. "I don't have a reason not to stick with you."

"That's hardly a ringing endorsement," she said.

"I like you Lydia, is that better?"

She smiled as she turned onto Cherry to cut down to 4th. "I've liked *you* since before I met you."

"I wouldn't take the things Ronnie says about me too seriously."

"I don't mean Ronnie."

Suddenly, every cell in my body was on alert. As casually as possible, I said, "You know one of my regulars from the bar?"

"No. Why don't you come into the office when we get there."

Five very uncomfortable minutes later, we were in Lydia's office. She took a book out of a drawer and lay it on her desk. One of those large, glossy paperbacks they like to make these days. Its title was *Operation Tea & Crumpets*. The picture on the cover was a photo of Chicago mobster Jimmy English done up to look like Andy Warhol had painted him. He hadn't. A cold sweat broke out on the back of my neck. I could tell it was going to be there a while. Long enough to mildew maybe.

"Have you read it?" Lydia asked. "It's pretty good."

"That's right. You like mobsters," I said, remembering something she'd said the night we met. "I should have taken that more seriously."

"The guy who wrote it is a friend of mine. Dickie Keswick. Richland now. Richland Keswick. He was Dickie in college. And much less pretentious."

"I never asked, how did you find Ronnie. Yellow pages?"

"As a matter of fact, Dickie recommended him."

I didn't ask how he might know Ronnie. I knew he didn't. He knew me and knew I was with Ronnie. She'd hired Ronnie to find her a house so she could get to me. I should have seen it. It was there in front of me all along, but I was too busy asking the wrong questions.

"You're the guy in the book, aren't you?"

"The guy in the book is Jimmy English. He's dead."

"Not him. The private eye. Nick Nowak."

"He's dead, too."

She stared at me. There was a kind of smirk on her face that, if she'd really understood the situation, wouldn't be there. "That's what it says in the book. That he's dead. But he isn't, is he?"

"He needs to be dead," I said.

"I don't see why."

"I'll be in danger. Ronnie will be in danger. I can't let that happen. If you won't leave this alone, I'll have to disappear."

Doubt flashed across her face. She began taking this seriously. "That's not really true—is it?"

"It is."

Sitting down behind her desk, a look came over her. One that I now recognized. She was looking at this from every angle. What was to be gained, what lost. What was true and what was not. After a long moment, she said, "All right. Nick Nowak is dead."

"Thank you."

"Don't thank me. I didn't kill him."

"No. I did."

EPILOGUE

Leap Year 1996
Thursday night

Danny Osborne sat on the edge of a king-sized bed on the twenty-fifth floor of the Bonaventure. As soon as he'd gotten into the room, as soon as they'd finally left him alone, he'd closed the drapes. Too much sky.

The other thing he'd done was take off his suit. It was cheap and didn't fit. The public defender who'd been there for his trial had bought it for him. He'd only worn it a handful of times.

In his underwear, he held the TV remote in his hand but didn't use it. There were more buttons than he remembered. Of course, they'd had television at Corcoran. He could watch whatever was on, but he never got to hold the remote. Never worked it.

Getting off the bed, he walked over to a door and opened it. The closet. The lawyer had bought him a couple of T-shirts and some socks and underwear. They sat on a shelf above the rods and hangers. The closet was around nine foot by six foot. He closed the door behind him and sat down in the dark.

ALSO BY MARSHALL THORNTON

IN THE BOYSTOWN MYSTERIES SERIES

The Boystown Prequels

(Little Boy Dead & Little Boy Afraid)

Boystown: Three Nick Nowak Mysteries

Boystown 2: Three More Nick Nowak Mysteries

Boystown 3: Two Nick Nowak Novellas

Boystown 4: A Time for Secrets

Boystown 5: Murder Book

Boystown 6: From the Ashes

Boystown 7: Bloodlines

Boystown 8: The Lies That Bind

Boystown 9: Lucky Days

Boystown 10: Gifts Given

Boystown 11: Heart's Desire

Boystown 12: Broken Cord

Boystown 13: Fade Out

IN THE PINX VIDEO MYSTERIES SERIES

Night Drop

Hidden Treasures

Late Fees

Rewind

Cash Out

OTHER BOOKS

The Perils of Praline

Desert Run

Full Release

The Ghost Slept Over

My Favorite Uncle

Femme

Praline Goes to Washington

Aunt Belle's Time Travel & Collectibles

Masc

Never Rest

The Less Than Spectacular Times of Henry Milch

Marshall Thornton writes two popular mystery series, the *Boystown Mysteries* and the *Pinx Video Mysteries*. He has won the Lambda Award for Gay Mystery three times. His romantic comedy, *Femme* was also a 2016 Lambda finalist for Best Gay Romance. Other books include *My Favorite Uncle, The Ghost Slept Over* and *Masc,* the sequel to *Femme*. He is a member of Mystery Writers of America.